orca limelights

Attitude

Robin Stevenson

ORCA BOOK PUBLISHERS

Library and Archives Canada Cataloguing in Publication

Stevenson, Robin, 1968-
Attitude / Robin Stevenson.
(Orca limelights)

Issued also in electronic format.
ISBN 978-1-4598-0382-4

I. Title. II. Series: Orca limelights
PS8637.T487A77 2013 jc813'.6 C2013-901908-1

First published in the United States, 2013
Library of Congress Control Number: 2013935387

Summary: Fitting in at her new ballet school turns out to be more painful for Cassie than breaking in a pair of pointe shoes.

Orca Book Publishers is dedicated to preserving the environment and has printed this book on Forest Stewardship Council® certified paper.

Orca Book Publishers gratefully acknowledges the support for its publishing programs provided by the following agencies: the Government of Canada through the Canada Book Fund and the Canada Council for the Arts, and the Province of British Columbia through the BC Arts Council and the Book Publishing Tax Credit.

Design by Teresa Bubela
Cover photography by Dreamstime

ORCA BOOK PUBLISHERS
PO Box 5626, Stn. B
Victoria, BC Canada
V8R 6S4

ORCA BOOK PUBLISHERS
PO Box 468
Custer, WA USA
98240-0468

www.orcabook.com
Printed and bound in Canada.

16 15 14 13 • 4 3 2 1

Dedicated, with much gratitude, to three inspiring young dancers: Sasha Beardmore, Alyssa Beattie and Sophia Harrington.

One

For as long as I can remember, ballet has been the center of my life. On our living room wall, there's a photo of me clutching the barre at my first class—a scrawny red-headed four-year-old in a black leotard, squinting out from behind blue plastic glasses. Since then, I've worked and sweated and stretched and strained through thousands of lessons and endless hours of practice. There is nothing in this world I want more than to be a dancer. What I'm doing right now should be—no, it *is*—a dream come true.

So why am I so scared?

I wrap my arms around myself, shivering under the thin gray airplane blanket, and tell myself sternly to smarten up.

Be strong, Cassandra, Peter told me at the end of class three nights ago.

You'll be fine, my mom said as she hugged me goodbye at the airport.

Better than fine, Dad said, winking at me. *Cassie's going to show those Canadian girls that Australians can dance.* And he cracked me up by attempting to do an arabesque and falling over right there in the departures area.

But now, as the plane bumps down onto the runway, a cold, empty feeling settles in the pit of my stomach, and I have to blink away my tears. I turn my face toward the window so the man in the next seat won't see me crying. The plane slows, turns and finally comes to a stop. I pretend to be very interested in the gray sky and the rain. It doesn't look much like summer.

I'm just arriving and already I am homesick. How am I going to cope with four weeks of this?

* * *

I've never traveled alone before, and I'm scared I will lose my passport or get lost, but I manage to get off the plane and find the baggage-claim area without any disasters. I had three stops on the way from my home in Adelaide, Australia, to my destination in Vancouver, Canada, so I'm getting used to airports. I feel numb and a little sick, but I'm not sure if it's from excitement or jet lag. I watch the suitcases and backpacks glide past on the conveyor belt and wish I could lie down on the floor and go to sleep right here.

I spot my blue duffel bag and heave it onto my shoulder. The weight of it is comforting—my dance clothes, three pairs of ballet slippers, my just-broken-in pointe shoes, my new jeans, a few photos of my friends and parents, and Jackie, my old stuffed bear. I wasn't going to bring him, but at the last minute I changed my mind and squeezed him in. I head through customs, scanning the crowd of people milling around the arrivals area, and it suddenly occurs to me that although my host family is supposed to be here to meet me, I have no idea how we will find each other. I hesitate, trying not to panic, and then I hear someone call my name.

I turn and see a tall dark-haired woman waving at me. The sign she is holding reads *WELCOME CASSANDRA JORDAN.* I blow out a tiny breath of relief and cross the short distance between us. Mrs. Harrison looks just like she did in the family photograph she emailed to us, slender and elegant in a flowing skirt and short fitted jacket. The long-haired girl standing beside her must be her daughter, Edie, who is fourteen—the same age as me.

"Cassandra. Welcome." Mrs. Harrison gives me a quick hug before leaning away and studying me, laughing. "We would have recognized you anywhere, wouldn't we, Edie?"

"You don't look much like your photograph," Edie says.

"I bet," I say ruefully. My photo is a glossy head shot—we had to send pictures as part of our application package to the school. "I'm a mess."

"I didn't mean that," Edie says, her cheeks turning pink.

"You look fine," Mrs. Harrison says briskly. "And I'd have spotted you even without that photograph. You look like a dancer, doesn't she, Edie?"

Edie nods but doesn't say anything.

Mrs. Harrison gives a short laugh. "Well, you do, Cassandra. It's the way you hold yourself.

Lovely posture." She takes my duffel bag from me. "Come on. I bet you're dying for a hot shower."

"Dying to go to bed, actually," I admit. "I've never been so tired in my life."

I follow them to the parking lot and slide into the back seat of their white minivan. Only twenty minutes to their house, Mrs. Harrison tells me. I sneak a glance at Edie's profile. She's pretty, with creamy skin and glossy dark hair like her mother, but she's not exactly chatty. She seems really shy. My thoughts are disjointed, dream-like. *Mrs. Harrison is beautiful. I wonder if my new host family has a dog. Dad looked so funny doing that arabesque at the airport, with his big belly sticking out. Classes start on Monday. I hope I like Canada...*

Next thing I know, Mrs. Harrison is touching my shoulder. "Cassandra? We're here."

I struggle out of a thick, heavy sleep. "Here?"

"Our house. Your new home for the summer." She smiles. "You were asleep before we hit the highway. You poor thing. I hated to wake you, but you can't sleep out in the driveway."

My curiosity about this place pushes the fog of sleep away like a strong breeze clearing clouds from the sky. I unbuckle my seat belt and get out of the car. Everything is green: the grass, the tidy bushes in the front yard, the tall trees that line the street. It is the beginning of July, which means it is summer here, but the sky is gray and the air is cool. Two days ago, when I left Australia, it was winter, but the weather was much the same: chilly, gray and raining.

No wonder I feel disoriented.

I follow Mrs. Harrison into the house, which is big and spotlessly clean but kind of boring—beige carpets and glass shelves and nature photographs on the off-white walls. "We've fixed up the spare room for you," she says, walking up the stairs. "Let's put your bag in there. David will be home from work soon and we'll have dinner. Do you feel like joining us, or do you really want to go to bed?"

"Probably better if I try and stay up, right?" I actually am kind of hungry.

"If you can bear it. You'll get over the jet lag faster that way." She puts my duffel bag on the floor at the foot of the bed. "There's a dresser for your clothes, and we put in a small bookshelf for you. I'm sorry it's such a small room."

"No, it's fine." There's a smooth wooden floor and enough room between the bed and dresser for me to do my stretches, and the bookshelf is the right height to use for balance. The walls are a soft pale blue, and a Degas ballerina print hangs above the bed. "Really." I smile at her. "It's great."

Mrs. Harrison gestures down the hallway. "If you want to freshen up, there's a bathroom on the right. Come on downstairs when you're ready. We'll eat in half an hour or so."

"Great. Thanks." I watch her leave, and as she closes the door behind her, my reflection swings into the full-length mirror on the back of my bedroom door. I stand and stare at myself for a minute. "This is it, Cassie," I whisper. "You're here. You're really here."

I stand tall, head lifted, back straight, shoulders down and back, and meet my eyes in the mirror. Underneath the messy dark hair, the tired pale face, the rumpled shirt, I can see her—the dancer I am going to be. Even though I am so tired I can barely stand up, I lift my arms and step into fifth position, and I feel strength and energy flooding through my limbs.

When I dance, I feel as if anything is possible.

Two

When I had first brought up the idea of applying to the Pacific Coast Ballet Academy, my parents hadn't liked the plan at all.

"You're only fourteen," Mom said. "Far too young to be away from home. And we'd miss you terribly." She reached across the table to put her hand on my arm, but I pulled away.

"Peter thinks I'd be a good candidate," I said. "And he thinks I'd learn a lot. Can't I at least audition for the summer program? I might not be accepted anyway."

"In Canada? That's awfully far away," Dad said.

"I know where Canada is." I made a face at him. "Can you at least look at the academy website? If I got accepted for the Summer Intensive, I'd be staying with a host family. And..." I take a deep breath. "If I did well...if they think I have potential...I could get invited to stay."

"What do you mean, stay? For how long?"

I looked down at my plate. "Um...a year."

"Cassie! A year?" Mom sounded like I had slapped her.

"What about school?" Dad asked.

"They set it all up for you." My words tumbled out in a rush of hope and excitement and guilt. "They've got it all worked out. I'd go to a regular high school all day, and then go to dance classes at the academy after school. If I got accepted, I mean. Which I probably wouldn't."

He shook his head. "Are you sure you want that? I know you love dancing, but that sounds like a tough workload. Anyway, why are they down here recruiting Australian dancers? Can't they find dancers in Canada?"

"Dad. Come on. It's an international school. I'd meet people—dancers—from all over the world. And they have a totally famous ballet company, and lots of their students end up joining it."

"But you wouldn't want to live there, would you? It's so far away..."

Canada might be far away, but the possibility of joining a ballet company felt even more distant. "I wouldn't have to," I said. "Seriously, their graduates get into all the best companies. I bet I could get into an Australian ballet company."

Mom leaned back and folded her arms across her chest. "That does sound interesting," she admitted. "But it's probably too expensive. And you've never really been away from home at all."

"I did that Girl Guide camp last summer," I said.

"And you hated it," Dad pointed out. "By the second day, you were begging to come home."

"This'd be different," I said. "None of my friends at school here understand why I even care about ballet so much. At the academy, we'd all be dancing together every day. We'd get to know each other. I'd make friends. And I'd be studying with great teachers." I squeezed my hands together, fingers laced, under my chin. "Please think about it?"

"It's not that we don't support you," Dad said. "You're a wonderful dancer. I just don't think your whole life should revolve around that one thing."

Mom nodded. "That's right. We want you to enjoy being a kid."

"I enjoy *dancing*," I said, fighting back tears. "And if I want to dance professionally, I *can't* wait until I'm older. It'll be too late."

They looked at each other. Mom sighed. Dad shrugged. "We'll think about it," they said, more or less in unison.

The next morning, Mom told me that they'd decided it was my choice. If I did the audition and got accepted for the Summer Intensive, I could go. Just for the summer. As for staying on in the fall, they said we'd cross that bridge when we came to it. I think maybe they expected me to change my mind, but I never even considered it. I knew what I wanted. I'm not usually overconfident, but somehow I knew it would happen. It just felt like it was meant to be.

And now, here I am, in my own room in a strange Canadian house with a family that I am going to be living with for four weeks. *Four weeks!* It sounds like forever. I change into a clean shirt, wash my face and brush my teeth, and head downstairs to join them for dinner.

The Harrisons are much more formal than my family. At home, we usually eat in the living room, in front of the TV, with our plates on our laps. Here, we sit at a table with a white tablecloth and pale-green place mats, and we have separate plates for salad and for the rest of our dinner, which is grilled fish and asparagus. I've never had asparagus before.

"So Cassandra," Mr. Harrison says, "I bet you have lots of questions for Edie."

He is smiling at me, and there is a glint of sympathy in his eye, like he understands how overwhelming this all is. I swallow a mouthful of food. "Um, yeah, I do, actually." I shift in my seat to face Edie, who is sitting beside me. "Have you been at the academy for a long time?"

"Since I was six," she says. Her voice is soft, barely more than a whisper. "I'm hoping to start PTP this fall."

"That's the Professional Training Program," Mrs. Harrison explains.

"That'd be amazing," I say. "You're lucky to live so close to such a great school."

She nods. "Are you just here for the summer? Or are you hoping to get into PTP?"

"I'd love to get in," I say. "But I don't know if my parents would let me stay. They might not want me to be away for that long." I look around the dining room, with its crystal chandelier and artwork on the walls, and think of my own comfy but slightly scruffy home. I can see it all so clearly in my mind—Muffin, my fat gray cat, curled up on Mom's lap; Dad dozing in his big chair in front of the TV; the enormous jigsaw puzzle we were working on still half-finished on the coffee table. There's a sudden ache in my throat. "A year's a really long time," I say.

I can see Edie relax as I say this. She actually smiles at me. "Well, the summer should be good," she says. "Hard work, but good."

"It'll be cool to meet other girls who love ballet as much as I do," I tell her. "Most of my friends back home thought I was crazy to spend so much time dancing."

"I dance ten hours a week," she says.

"Same here, I guess. Ballet three times a week, and tap and jazz once each."

Edie takes a sip of water. "My best friend at the school—Melissa—she's going to get into PTP for sure. She's an incredible dancer. The teachers all love her. Her mom was a dancer, a famous one. She danced the lead parts in *Swan Lake, Giselle, Romeo and Juliet*...practically every ballet you can think of."

"That's amazing." I smile at her. Now that we're talking about ballet, Edie is like a different person.

"Edie's mother used to dance too," Mr. Harrison tells me. "When she and the girls get talking about ballet, it's like they're speaking another language."

Mrs. Harrison laughs. "I took some lessons as a kid," she says. "I didn't ever get close to the level you girls are at now."

Edie nods. "Melissa's mother was in a whole other league. Like, a prima ballerina."

"Wow," I say. "That'd be so cool, to have a famous ballet dancer for a mom."

Mrs. Harrison slides a bowl of whole-grain rolls toward me. "A lot to live up to, I would imagine."

"I guess so." My mom says she dances like a chicken with two left feet. No pressure there. Quite the opposite, actually. She thinks I'm crazy for wanting to dance as much as I do. "Tell me more about the Professional Training Program," I say.

Edie balances her chin on her fingertips. "In PTP, you dance, like, twenty hours a week. The academy has this arrangement with the high schools so you get to leave early and dance every day for at least four hours. And that's not including rehearsal for recitals and festivals and stuff like that. That's just your regular dance classes."

"Edie, elbows off the table," Mrs. Harrison says.

I realize my own elbows are on the table too and hastily sit back and place my hands in my lap. "How many girls will get in?"

Edie shrugs. "Not as many as are hoping to. It's probably a good thing you're planning to go home at the end of the summer session."

I nod and grin, but inside me, hope and ambition are leaping up and dancing a crazy pas de deux.

"It can get a bit intense," Mrs. Harrison says. "The summer session is really a four-week-long audition, isn't it, Edie? Especially for the new girls. It gives the teachers a chance to really assess who has the potential for a career as a dancer. Physically and mentally."

"Courage, passion, dedication," Edie says, as if she is quoting, and I recognize the words from the academy website.

I know I have the passion. I am pretty sure I have the dedication. But do I have the courage to become a dancer if it means leaving my family?

Three

Mrs. Harrison drops Edie and me off at the academy on Monday morning. "I'm sorry I can't come in with you, Cassandra," she says. "I'm running late for work, but Edie will show you around and introduce you to everyone."

I pick up my bag and slide out of the car. "I'll be fine." Edie is already halfway to the front doors, and I hurry to catch up and follow her inside.

Girls are milling about in black leotards and tights, duffel bags slung over shoulders, shiny hair scraped up into tight buns. My heart is beating fast. I lift my chin, determined not to let anyone see how nervous I am. Edie takes me to the office, where an older woman with dyed-black hair and a lot of gold jewelry checks my name off a list. "Studio Three," she says. "Cassandra will start off with you,

Edie, so you can show her where to go. Here are name tags for you both. Just pin them to your leotards, please."

Edie nods and guides me down the crowded hallway, up a flight of stairs and through another set of doors. I can feel myself calm down as I step into the studio. With the mirrored wall, the double bar and the piano in the corner, it feels just like my dance classes back home. Girls are already sitting on the floor, stretching, adjusting their shoes and chatting.

"Melissa!" Edie runs forward and throws her arms around a tall slender girl with flaming red hair. "I've missed you."

Melissa laughs. "Goof. I was only away for a week."

"I know, but..." She trails off and turns to me. "This is Cassie. She's our homestay student."

"Hello, Cassie." Melissa eyes me appraisingly for a long moment, then turns back to Edie. "There's a lot of new girls, have you noticed?"

"Are there? We just got here," Edie says. She looks around the room and I follow her gaze, feeling a little dismayed at the size of the group. At home, there were never more than fifteen or so in a class, but there must be close to thirty girls in here. Some seem very young, not more than eleven, I'd guess; others look maybe sixteen or even older. Everyone is dressed the same—black leotards, soft shoes, the palest pink tights.

"Good morning, girls!" A teacher walks to the front of the room, and the chatter and giggling subside. She waits for complete silence before she begins. "Welcome to the first day of the Summer Intensive. I am Diana Komlos—you can call me Diana—and I teach ballet and contemporary here at the academy. We're going to be working hard over these next four weeks, and I am expecting you all to give one hundred percent."

"Yes, Diana," some of the girls say.

Diana is about thirty and quite elegant, with a long slender neck and white-blond hair tied back in a short ponytail instead of a bun. She speaks slowly and clearly, her eyes moving from one of us to another, and I can sense that she is already assessing us. "Martha Graham once said that dance is the hidden language of the soul," she says. "Think about that, girls. The body doesn't lie."

I wait, barely breathing, wanting to hold on to every word. I feel like she can see right into me.

I drop my shoulders, lift my chin, pull in my stomach and hope that she sees whatever it is she is looking for.

She smiles. "For this first class, we're going to be taking things a little more slowly than we usually do," she says. "I want to see where you are all at and what you can do, so that I know what we need to work on. Mrs. Hoffman, another one of our teachers, will be observing the first half of our class." She gestures toward an older dark-haired woman standing just inside the door, and the woman nods at us without smiling. "I'll be dividing you into three smaller groups, and I'll let you know what those groups will be at the end of this class."

Melissa and Edie exchange looks, no doubt hoping they will be in the same group. I cross my fingers for a moment, hoping I'll be with them and not a bunch of complete strangers.

"Let's get started," Diana says, clapping her hands briskly. "Positions at the barre, everyone. First position, please."

I take a place at the barre behind Edie and Melissa. The smooth wood under my hand feels comfortingly familiar, and I take a deep breath before settling into the routine exercises. *First position. Heels together. Turn out from the hip.*

"Think of trees," Diana says. "Think of how they reach up for the sunlight, trying to be the tallest tree. Lift your abdomen, straighten your spine. From the hipbones up, be like a tree, stretching up." She stands behind one girl, holding her hand an inch or so above her head. "Stretching to touch my hand...yes." She walks on, past me, and our eyes meet in the mirror for a second. "What else do trees have?" she asks me.

"Roots?" I say.

"Yes. Trees also have roots. So below the hipbones, stretching down into the ground, sending your roots deep to find the water... good."

I focus on the stretch in my muscles, trying to get as much turnout as I can, making sure my position is perfect.

"Iako, lovely turnout. Heels together, though—don't be sloppy. Edie, drop your shoulders." Diana walks down the line, pausing to correct each girl as she passes. "Julie, turn out from the hip. Nice work, Zoe, but tuck your seat in. Cassandra, make sure you keep your shoulders level." She touches my left shoulder, pressing down lightly. "Okay, now demi-plié."

I bend my knees slowly, concentrating on keeping my thighs turned out.

"Heels stay on the floor, Julie." Diana approaches the girl behind me. "That's it. Make sure those heels stay together." She raises her voice to address us all. "And grand plié!"

I take a deep breath, let my heels lift and bend my knees farther, sinking into a grand plié.

"Very nice..." She pauses, bending to look at my name tag. "Very nice, Cassandra. Julie, a little deeper, bring your thighs parallel to the floor... that's it. And slowly come up again, back into first position. Slowly, Edie! Don't rush." Diana nods at me as she passes. "Good, Kendra, good...Zoe, bring your heels back to the floor as soon as you can. Let's see that again...yes, plié, and now rising up... heels, heels...hmm. A little better, Zoe."

Over the next hour, Diana takes us through a series of exercises at the barre: tendus, retirés, développés, pirouettes, arabesques and attitudes. There is a level of seriousness and intensity in the room that is pushing me to work even harder than usual. My legs are trembling, and I know I'll be sore tomorrow.

Finally the class is over and we are stretching, warming down. "Shake it out," Diana says. "Shake it out."

Edie leans toward me. "What did you think?" she whispers.

"It was excellent," I say. "She's awesome."

"She's a good teacher. I hope I'm in her group."

"Me too." I know without a doubt that studying with Diana is going to make me a better dancer.

Diana is making notes on a clipboard as we pull on hoodies and slip off our shoes. Finally she looks up. "I'm sure you are all dying to know your groups for the summer. Do some stretches until ten o'clock—that'll give me a few minutes to finalize the lists. I'll post them on the bulletin board in the downstairs hall. Any questions, please let me know."

Diana leaves and we all stretch, doing splits and flexing our feet, but no one's mind is on the exercises. Everyone's talking and laughing, and as soon as the clock on the wall says ten, the rest of the class rushes past me, out into the hall and down the stairs. I hang back on the landing for a moment, adjusting my crooked name tag and watching them descend. From above, all I can see is the tops of their heads—dozens of girls with smooth hair pulled into tight buns. My legs are tired, but I am suddenly filled with energy, my muscles loose and springy, and I feel like I could jump right up to the ceiling, lifted by sheer excitement.

I run down the stairs and join the crowd at the bulletin board. Edie grabs my arm. "You're with us," she says. "In Diana's group, with me and Melissa."

"Good," I say, relieved.

Melissa raises one eyebrow. "They did it mostly by age, really. All the eleven- and twelve-year-olds are together in one group, then there's our group, then the older girls."

"We don't know how old the new girls are," Edie points out.

Melissa shrugs. "*Mostly* by age, I said. Anya, Danika, Zoe, you, me, Cassie—we're all thirteen or fourteen or fifteen."

I'm trying to remember the names and failing miserably. "How many of our group are new?" I ask.

"Lots," Edie says. "That girl Iako, she's new."

"And the American girl," Melissa says. "You know. The one with no bun."

"Oh yeah. Cam, I think." I had noticed her, and glanced at her name tag, because her dark brown hair is really short. She is tall and freckled, and her short hair looks cute. Still, it is an odd choice for a dancer, and I wonder how she will manage it for performances.

"A couple of others, too. There are ten in our group altogether," Melissa says, counting on her fingers. "The five of us who belong here plus Cassie and four other new girls." She looks at me and her eyes narrow; then she turns back to Edie. "Did you notice how the teachers fuss over the new girls? They totally got all the attention."

"Well, I guess the teachers already know the rest of us," Edie says.

Melissa ignores her, beckoning imperiously to a group of dancers standing farther down the hall. Three girls approach us, the third leaping into a temps levé in arabesque as she moves across the floor. "Danika, Zoe, Anya—have you guys met Cassie? She's staying with Edie."

They all nod and say hi, and I know I'm going to get the three of them mixed up. I'm really bad with names and faces. Melissa's red hair is a gift, but Anya, Danika and Zoe all have long brown hair pulled back tightly into buns. *Zoe has braces,* I tell myself. *Anya has streaky blond highlights. Danika is the small one with diamond stud earrings...*

"So," Melissa says, "how many of us do you think will get invited to stay in the fall?"

Zoe shrugs. "They'll take more from the older group, probably."

Danika nods, her expression thoughtful. "From our group just two or three, I bet."

"That's it?" I say, dismayed. "Two out of ten?"

"At best," Melissa says darkly. "But I can tell you right now, it won't be Iako or Miss No-Bun. So really, it's more like two out of eight." She extends one leg, toes pointed and stretched out in front of her. *Tendu devant,* I think automatically.

Edie giggles. "It's like a TV show, you know? Like *Survivor.*"

Danika laughs, and Zoe lowers her voice to imitate a reality-show host. "The tribe has spoken."

Melissa looks thoughtful. She lowers her foot to the ground. "Summer session is four weeks. So if eight people have to go, that's two a week."

"Oh, come on." I laugh, but I feel uneasy. "That's not how it works. I mean, no one's voting people off."

"Sure they are," Melissa says. "I bet Diana and Mrs. Hoffman are talking about us right now." She puts on a fake German accent. "Zat leetle girl—ze Chinese girl, Iako—she doesn't have the drive, the passion. She gives up too easily."

"I'm pretty sure she's from Japan," I say. "Not China."

"Same difference," Melissa says.

"No, actually—" I start to speak, but she cuts me off.

"The point is, Cassandra, that Iako was practically crying at the end of the class because it was too hard. Her hip was hurting." She smirks. "A dancer has to be strong. If she can't handle a little pain, how's she going to cope with being a professional dancer?"

Anya nods. "We should vote her off right now."

"It's not our decision," I tell Melissa. My heart is beating faster than usual, and I wish this conversation wasn't happening. The last thing I want to do is make enemies. "I mean, we can vote if you want, but everyone will still be here."

"Will they?" Melissa's voice is sharp, and her blue eyes are icy.

I can feel the hairs on the back of my neck lifting, prickling. "Well, yeah, of course. And who says Diana and Mrs. Hoffman will agree with your choices? It's their votes that will count in the end."

She ignores me. "Show of hands. Who thinks Iako isn't cut out for this? Who is ready to vote her off?"

And all around me, the hands go up. Melissa. Edie. Anya. Zoe. Danika. I clasp my own hands together behind my back. "Cassie?" Edie nudges me, her eyes wide and anxious. "Aren't you voting?"

I know Iako has as much right to be here as any of us. And I know what my dad would say: *Just do what you know is right, Cassie, and everything else will fall into place.*

But a small voice in my head is screaming at me: *You're putting a target on your own back, Cassandra! Just go along with it!* Because I can tell that Melissa is the queen bee around here, and making her mad is probably a really bad idea.

Especially since I have to live with her best friend for the next four weeks.

Besides, it won't really hurt Iako if I vote. The whole thing is stupid, but it's just a game, after all—it's not like these votes actually count toward anything.

I lift my hand, and Edie grins at me. I smile back, but there's a sick feeling in my gut. Maybe they'd understand, but I know my parents wouldn't be proud of me right now.

"That's six votes," Melissa says. "Iako's history."

Four

After a short break, the ten of us are taken to have our pointe shoes checked and get new shoes if we need them. Mrs. Hoffman, who is friendlier now than she seemed earlier, takes us into a small room lined from floor to ceiling with shelves and filled with more ballet shoes than I've seen in my life.

We sit on a long bench to wait our turn. I'm sitting in the middle, and Mrs. Hoffman is slowly working her way down the line. On my left are all the girls who just voted against Iako. Danika is holding out a foot for Mrs. Hoffman to inspect, Anya and Zoe are watching, and Edie is whispering with Melissa, her back turned toward me. On my right are Iako and the three other new girls. The short-haired girl, Cam, grins at me.

I start to smile back. Then I remember that she's going to be next on Melissa's list, and a wave of hot shame makes me drop my eyes.

Mrs. Hoffman has moved on to Anya and is fussing over her shoes. "Tch, tch. These are getting worn out. You're not getting much support from this box anymore."

Anya groans. "I've only had them three weeks."

The teacher nods. "You can use some jet glue to stiffen it, maybe get a little more use from them, but you really need new ones." She hands the shoe back and moves on to Zoe. "Ah yes, this foot I remember."

Zoe makes a face. "Why do I feel like that isn't a good thing?"

"Your second toe's longer than your big toe. Looks like you've been getting blisters on that middle joint, yes?"

"Always. Well, for the last two years anyway. Since I started on pointe."

I look down at Zoe's foot and notice that her middle toes are wrapped in white tape. I started on pointe two years ago, but for the first year I didn't do much at all. Anya's worn-out shoes and Zoe's taped toes make me wonder if the other girls all have more experience than I do.

Mrs. Hoffman moves on down the line, commenting on Melissa's feet. "Beautiful, beautiful. Lovely flexible feet, and look at that instep!" She pushes down on Melissa's foot, increasing the curve, and I can't help agreeing that it's beautiful. "Take care of these high arches, dear. You'll have to work to keep them strong. Remind me to give you some exercises."

"You've given me them before," Melissa says.

"And are you doing them?"

"Yes. Well...sometimes."

"Every day," Mrs. Hoffman says firmly. "A beautiful foot is no use if you cannot dance on it, and without strong feet, you cannot dance."

She checks Edie's shoes and nods approval, and then stands in front of me. "Now for the new girls. Let's see your feet, dears, and make sure your shoes are fitting properly."

I lift my right foot, and she takes it in her cool hands, flexing my arch, pushing down on my toes, feeling my ankle and heel. "A lovely neat foot," she says and glances at my name tag. "See this, girls? Cassandra's big toe and the next two toes are all the same length. Very square, this foot. This means that when she goes on pointe, her weight will be distributed across the three toes."

My cheeks warm with both pleasure and embarrassment—I hear Melissa whisper something, and a couple of the other girls snicker. Mrs. Hoffman doesn't seem to notice. "Put these back on and let's see you on pointe."

I slip my shoes back on, lace them around my ankles, stand up and rise onto my toes.

Mrs. Hoffman squats, inspecting my feet. "Your shoes fit nicely, dear, but keep your feet straight. See this? You're a little out on your baby toes. We call that sickling, and you don't want to do that. The space between your feet needs to stay equal, yes?" She rests her fingers on the outsides of my heels, pressing lightly. "Like so. You must have nice straight feet."

I nod. "Thanks."

She smiles at me as I sit back down, then moves on to Iako. "May I see your foot, dear?"

Iako holds out her foot silently. I watch her, feeling uncomfortable. "A beautiful foot," Mrs. Hoffman says, and Iako smiles uncertainly.

"Very flexible," Mrs. Hoffman continues. "That's good. Now put the shoes on and let's check the fit."

"Sorry? I don't...can you..." Iako's cheeks are pink. "My English..."

I can hear Edie and Melissa whispering.

"Put on the shoes," Mrs. Hoffman says again. "And stand up, dear."

Iako nods, puts her shoes on and goes on pointe so smoothly and quickly that it appears as natural as standing flat-footed. She has long thin legs and looks like she was born on her toes.

"These shoes are a little too big for you, yes? The shank extends slightly beyond your heel."

Iako nods and sits back down, but I'm not sure she understood. I can't imagine how hard it must be for her—she is as far from home as I am, and on top of that, she has to communicate in a foreign language. I feel a flash of anger—at Melissa, for targeting someone who probably could use some friends, and at myself, for going along with it.

"Try these," Mrs. Hoffman says, passing her another pair, which Iako puts on. "Stand again." She holds out a hand, gesturing for Iako to rise onto her toes again. "Yes, yes. Better." She pats Iako on the shoulder. "Very good. Make sure you break them in properly. You know how, yes?" She demonstrates, kneading the box with her fingers and flexing the shank. Iako nods, gives her a grateful smile and sits back down.

Edie nudges me. "She can't even speak English."

"So?" I say. "We can't speak Japanese."

"Of course not. But we're not trying to go to a ballet school in Japan, are we?"

"I think she's brave," I say. "Don't you?"

She hesitates. "I guess so. Sort of."

I watch as Mrs. Hoffman nods approval over Cam's feet and the fit of her shoes and fusses a little over Julie's. "Tch, tch. Not the most flexible foot, is it, dear? You can't do much about the height of your arch, but I'll give you some exercises to do."

"I know," Julie says ruefully. She looks younger than the rest of the group and has curly fair hair that keeps springing free of her bun. "My teacher back home says I have flat feet."

"Well, yes, but flat feet can be strong feet. You work with what you have. Margot Fonteyn didn't have high arches and it didn't hinder her career, did it?"

Julie laughs. "Exactly what my teacher always says."

"It's quite true. Feet like Melissa's, with a high instep and high arch, create beautiful lines and have the flexibility for great jumps, but if you don't work hard and do your exercises"—she shoots Melissa a look—"they can also be prone to injury." And with that she moves on to the last girl in the line, Mackenzie, who is a light-skinned black girl, small but very strong.

Edie nudges me again. "Have lunch with me and Melissa, okay?"

"Okay."

"Melissa overheard some of the teachers talking," she says. "There's going to be an audition coming up."

"An audition?" I lower my voice. "For what?"

"*The Nutcracker*," she whispers. "Guess what role."

"Not Clara."

"Yup. Clara. Actually, they're looking for *two* Claras."

I blow out a long slow breath. *The Nutcracker*. I fell in love with ballet as a four-year-old after I saw *The Nutcracker* on television. I've even had small parts in it back home, once as a mouse and once as a soldier. To dance the part of Clara would be a dream come true. But... "That's not until Christmas, though, right?"

"Yeah. So I guess you won't be here."

"I might be here," I say. "I mean, I'd kind of like to stay."

She rolls her eyes. "You'd *kind of like to*?"

"I want to stay," I say, meaning it. "I do."

"Well, we'll see," she says, frowning slightly. "I'll talk to Melissa."

I think of what my dad always says—*you get out what you put in*. I've always believed that my success depends entirely on me—my courage, my passion, my determination to dance—but Edie's words and tone of voice scare me.

She makes it sound as if my fate rests entirely in someone else's hands.

Five

The gray clouds that hung low all weekend have cleared, and it's a gorgeous, sunny day. Edie and I take our lunch bags outside and sit on the grass. We both have lunches packed by her mom: turkey sandwiches, carrot sticks, sliced peaches. The Harrisons are very health conscious; they'd be horrified if they peeked into our kitchen cupboards back home. Mrs. Harrison says proper nutrition is important if you want to be a dancer, and I guess that's probably true, but I sure miss steak pies and ice cream.

Edie glances at her watch. "I don't know what's taking Melissa so long," she says. "She was just getting a drink from the vending machine..." She breaks off. "Here she comes."

Melissa jogs across the grass and drops down beside us. She sits with her legs in the splits, stretching. "Pointe class after lunch," she says. "How long have you been on pointe, Cassandra?"

"Two years," I say. Going on pointe was something I'd started begging to do when I was eleven, but Peter had said my feet were still growing and that rushing pointe work could be damaging. When I turned twelve, he finally said my feet and ankles were strong enough. I was excited about my first pointe class, but, I have to admit, it was disappointing. Just a few minutes of exercises, and I'd been on the verge of tears from the pain and frustration. It was so much harder than it looked. After that, I'd spent countless hours stretching and strengthening my feet. When I watched TV, I did resistance exercises with my toes pushed against a stretchy latex band. When I brushed my teeth or waited for the school bus, I did foot flexes. In class, I worked at the barre practicing rises, relevés and échappés, and I waited impatiently to go into the center of the room and actually *dance.* Peter had finally started letting me do a little more, but I'd still felt impatient. I wanted to do everything that the older girls did.

Of course, now I am one of those older girls, dancing on pointe—and I still wish I could do more. I still ache to dance like the senior dancers.

Edie smiles at me. "Two years? That's the same as me," she says.

Melissa takes a sip of water and looks at me over her water bottle. "When I started coming here three years ago, I was already on pointe. I started at ten."

"Wow." When I was ten, I used to fantasize about pointe shoes and try to stand on my toes in my sneakers, but I'd been nowhere near ready. "That's pretty young."

Melissa shrugs. "My teacher at my old school said I was exceptionally strong for my age. Here, they don't usually start before twelve though, so you won't be too far behind most of the girls. Did you do the Cecchetti exams in Australia?"

"Yes." I take a bite of my sandwich. "I'll do my grade six in December. Unless, you know, I'm still here." I meet her eyes. "Edie says you heard that there might be an audition for *The Nutcracker.*"

"I heard Mrs. Hoffman talking to one of the other teachers when I was down at the office.

She said they were looking at the girls in PTP for Clara. Then she said that maybe some of the summer session girls could audition too. " Melissa looks around, making sure that no one is close enough to overhear. "I'd better be one of them."

"Me too," Edie says quickly.

"I'll make sure I am," Melissa says.

I laugh. "But how can you? I mean, isn't it up to the teachers?"

She makes a dismissive gesture. "You either want to be a dancer or you don't, Cassandra. And if you want it, then you do whatever it takes."

I don't quite trust Melissa. Then again, a chance to dance Clara... "I want it," I say.

"Good." Her thin face splits in a wide smile. "Smart choice, Cassandra."

There is an uneasy sensation in my belly. I feel like I've just agreed to something that I don't quite understand, and I'm still worrying about it half an hour later as we're filing into the studio for pointe class.

"Places at the barre!" Diana calls out.

I'm first to the barre, and I take the front spot, figuring I won't be distracted there by watching and comparing myself to everyone else.

Edie nudges me. "Um, Cassandra? Melissa always stands at the front of the barre."

"Oh. Sure. Sorry." Flustered, I step aside and let Melissa take my place. Edie squeezes in behind her, leaving no room for me.

"There's room over here," Cam calls, and I join her near the back. "What was that about?" she asks in a low voice.

"I guess Melissa has dibs on that front spot," I say.

"So you stood aside for her." Cam shrugs. "It's your call, of course..."

"But?"

She raises her eyebrows. "I know we only just got here, but I get the impression that Melissa is used to being number one."

"Yeah. Well, she's great, isn't she?"

"She's a good dancer," Cam says carefully.

I think she might say more, but Diana is already calling out directions.

"First position, please, girls. Elongate your spine, eyes forward...Julie, turnout from the hip... and start the rise onto the balls of your feet, into the highest demi-pointe you can...that's right, Zoe, nice...and pushing up into full pointe...

and releasing back to demi-pointe...and back into first position." She walks over and taps my bum. "Tuck, Cassandra. Squeeze."

I tighten my muscles.

"Again. Demi-pointe...full pointe...and back to first. Mackenzie, it should be a smooth, fluid motion. Melissa, can you demonstrate?"

Melissa does a series of pointe exercises, with Diana pointing out her excellent turnout and the alignment of her feet. "Now let's see the rest of you try it again. No sickling your feet, remember! Nice and straight!"

I don't know what Melissa is planning to do to make sure she gets to audition, but it seems to me that the part of Clara will be hers if she wants it.

"Julie, that's better. Cam, too much weight on your baby toe, you're on the corner of the box—there, that's it, that's better—" Diana breaks off. "Where's Iako?"

We all stop and look around. "I saw her at lunchtime," Cam says. "She didn't say anything about missing class."

"Hmm." Diana frowns.

"Shall I check the washroom?" Cam offers.

"Yes. Thank you, Cam." Diana claps her hands. "Okay. Second position, girls. Julie, turn out from the hip, not the knee."

I try to focus on my position, but I can't concentrate. This morning, Melissa and the other girls—including me, I think, with a flush of guilt—voted Iako off. And now she's gone. *It has to be a coincidence,* I tell myself. *Melissa can't make people disappear...*

"Cassandra! Are you paying attention?" Diana's voice is sharp.

"Sorry," I say, realizing that everyone is doing relevés in fifth position and I am still standing here flat-footed.

"Don't jump onto pointe, girls. A smooth motion. Cassandra, if I asked you to let go of the barre right now, I think you'd fall over."

She's right. I'm off balance. I hastily adjust my position and check my reflection in the mirror.

"Cassandra, look at the waistband on your leotard," she says. "See that straight line? It should be level. Make sure your hips are even...there! That's better." Diana watches for a moment, and then tells us all to stop. "It isn't magic," she says. "It's technique. It's all technique. Balance is easy when your body is in the right position. Try again. Tailbone directly over the ball of your foot. Lift your abdomen. Long straight spine."

"Diana?" Cam is standing in the doorway with her arm around Iako, who has clearly been crying. "Iako's pointe shoes. She was given new ones this morning, but they seem to have disappeared from her gym bag."

"Are you sure you didn't leave them somewhere?" Diana asks.

Iako wipes her arm across her eyes. "I think... someone took them."

Diana frowns. "That seems rather unlikely, Iako." She sighs. "Please go and see Mrs. Hoffman and get another pair. Quickly."

Iako nods and scurries off like a scared mouse.

I look at my reflection in the mirror. My turnout isn't bad—my position is pretty close to perfect—but it all feels a bit forced and mechanical. The elastic springy feeling in my legs is gone, and the music isn't filling me with energy the way it usually does. *Come on, Cassandra,* I whisper under my breath. *You came here to dance, so dance.*

But when I look into my eyes, I don't see a dancer. All I see is fear.

* * *

When Iako returns to class, her eyes are puffy and her face is flushed from crying. She gets her shoes on and joins us at the barre, but her concentration is shot. Diana keeps telling her to focus and pay attention. As we leave the studio at the end of class, I notice she is limping, and I realize she hadn't even had a few minutes to break in her new shoes. The box must still be hard as stone.

"Iako!" I call out to her impulsively.

"Yes?" With her spindly legs and wide dark eyes, she looks like a startled fawn.

"Um, are you okay?"

She nods. "Thank you. Yes. I am okay."

"I'm from Australia," I say. "So I figure you and me—well, we're both a long way from home."

"It is hard," she says. "But it is good to be here."

"Yes." I hesitate. "I'm sorry about what happened. With your shoes."

Her eyebrows pull together in a frown. "I do not understand it," she says. "I know they were in my bag." She gestures helplessly. "But I am so tired. I must have forgotten. The jet lag, you know?"

"I know. I keep waking up at, like, three in the morning." Way down the hall, I can see Edie and Melissa staring at us. "I should go," I say. "I just wanted to say—well, you dance beautifully."

She smiles and suddenly looks older and more confident. "It is my life," she says.

Six

That evening, I borrow Edie's laptop and Skype my parents. I have to wait until almost bedtime to call them because Vancouver time is so far behind the time at home. I'm in my pajamas, but in Adelaide it's five o'clock tomorrow afternoon. It's weird to think about. As soon as my mom's face appears on the screen, I feel a wave of homesickness so bad I just about break down and cry.

"Cassie! Wait a sec, honey. I'll call your dad." She steps away from the camera, and I can see the living room couch and the cluttered bookshelves behind it. "Mike! It's Cassie!" she yells, and a moment later both of them are there, crowding close to the camera and grinning widely.

"How are you guys?" It's hard to talk—there's a lump the size of Tasmania in my throat. "I miss you," I say.

"We're fine, fine," Mom says. "Tell us all about it. Are you okay? Not too homesick? How's the dancing?"

"It's good," I say. "The teacher—Diana—she's excellent. And guess what? There's going to be an audition for *The Nutcracker*! They're looking for a Clara. At least, that's the rumor."

"Wow, that's great," Dad says.

"Isn't that a Christmas production though?" Mom asks.

"Um, yeah." There's a long silence, and then I stumble on. "I mean, I probably won't get the part. There are a lot of girls here who are really good."

"Including you, Cassie," Dad says.

"You are good," Mom agrees. "Actually, I just ran into Peter—"

"You saw Peter? Really?" I miss him, too. He's thirty or so but very good-looking, so a lot of the older girls have crushes on him. He's like a big brother to me though. He's been teaching me since I was nine.

"At the grocery store," Mom says. "He was raving about you."

"Seriously?"

"Seriously. He said you were very talented."

"Mom, did he use that word? Or is that your interpretation?"

She laughs. "Don't you trust me?"

"I do, I just wanted to know what he said. Exactly, I mean." Peter doesn't give a lot of compliments to his students. A "well done" from him is high praise.

"Well, he did use that word. No, wait, let me think. He said you had real talent and *innate musicality*." She makes air quotes with her fingers.

I savor the warm glow those words give me and feel my cheeks getting hot. "Diana—our teacher here—she says that dance is the hidden language of the soul."

"Whatever that means," Dad says. He's grinning, though, like he really does understand.

"I think it means...I think it's about how, when you dance, you're expressing who you really are," I say.

"Ah well, you should be a star, then," Dad says.

I make a face at them both. "I miss you guys," I say again.

"We miss you too," Mom says. "But it won't be long. Just four weeks. It'll be over before you know it."

My eyes sting, and I think I might cry.

"You just do your thing," Dad says. "Dance your heart out. Do some pliés and some of those cheese things."

I laugh despite the tears that are threatening to spill over. "Cheese things?"

"You know. Fondues."

"Dad!" He knows exactly what fondus are. And frappés, which he pretends to think come from Starbucks. It's been a running joke between us for years.

He chuckles. "You'll be fine, Cassie. Just have fun."

"Call us again soon," Mom says.

I nod and say goodbye. I wish I could ask them what they think about all the stuff that is going on with the other girls, but it's too hard to explain.

Now, sitting cross-legged on my bed and staring at my own reflection in the dark screen of the laptop, I can't stop worrying. Did Iako really misplace her shoes? Or did Edie and Melissa have a hand in it? I pick up Jackie, my bear, and squeeze him tightly.

There's a knock on the door, and Edie pokes her head in. "Are you still Skyping your parents?"

"No. I'm done." I shove Jackie behind me and close the computer. "What's up?"

"Nothing. Just wondering what you thought about your first day at the academy." She balances on one foot, her left hand resting on the doorknob, and does an attitude—like an arabesque, with one foot extended behind her, but with her leg bent at the knee and lifted high. The line of her back and her leg are beautiful, and her turnout is excellent. She makes the position look as easy and natural as standing on two feet.

"You're so flexible," I say. "That's awesome."

"I used to do a lot of gymnastics," she says. "I loved it, actually, but it was hard to do both. Too much time, you know? Mom said I had to pick one or the other."

"Was it hard to choose?"

"Not really. I miss gymnastics, but giving up ballet wasn't an option, you know?"

"Yeah. I know. Ballet's my whole life." And I remember Iako saying the same thing earlier today: *It is my life.* I swallow hard and force myself to look at Edie. "You know what happened today with Iako?"

"Oh my god, I know. I guess Melissa was right about her." She brings her foot back to the ground and slides to the floor into the splits. "I mean, who shows up for a pointe class without pointe shoes?"

I hesitate. "So Melissa didn't have anything to do with it?"

Edie stares at me. "What do you mean?"

"I just wondered. I thought maybe, because of voting her off..."

"What, that she took her shoes or something?" She looks horrified. "Of course not. It's just a game, right? The voting thing."

"Is it?"

"Of course. She wouldn't actually steal someone's shoes." She swings her legs together and stands up. "I can't believe you'd think that, Cassandra. I mean, she's my best friend."

"I didn't really think she'd do that," I say quickly. "It was just a weird coincidence." I feel a wave of relief. Iako had told me she was jet-lagged and exhausted. She must have just misplaced the shoes. I grin at Edie. "Today was awesome. Tough, but awesome. I loved it."

She grins back. "Good. Because tomorrow's going to be even more awesome. And even tougher."

Seven

As soon as I get out of bed, I can feel the soreness in my muscles from yesterday's dancing. I limp downstairs for breakfast, calf muscles and thighs aching, and eat my cereal across the table from Edie. "Are you stiff today?" I ask her.

"No. Are you?"

Edie's hair is already pinned up, and she is clear-eyed and wide awake. I'm still in my pajamas and feel like I've been run over by a bus. Maybe it's the jet lag. "Not too bad," I say, wondering how on earth I am going to get through today's classes.

After breakfast, I dress and do some stretching in my bedroom. It helps, a little, and my muscles loosen up as the day goes on. By the end of the first class—modern dance, which I haven't done much of before but which is totally fun—I'm feeling almost back to normal.

"Nice work, girls," Diana says. "And now I have an announcement for you—some news I think you will all find rather exciting. I was speaking this morning with Andrew Kingsley, from our very own Pacific Coast Ballet."

There is a hum of excitement all around me as girls whisper to each other.

"As some of you know, our local ballet company does a number of productions every year. Most of the dancers are from within the company, but sometimes they need child dancers. They'll be holding open auditions—"

"*The Nutcracker*!" Julie bursts out. "Is it? Are they doing *The Nutcracker*?"

Diana holds up a hand for silence, but she is laughing. "Yes, Julie. That's exactly what they are doing. They're looking for young kids to play the parts of the mice, the party girls, the angels and the soldiers. I imagine lots of our beginners will be auditioning."

We all wait, holding our breath.

She smiles. "And they also have something for you girls in our intermediate classes.

Because of the number of performances and the amount of dancing required—they'll be doing the show in two locations—they're looking for two girls to play the part of Clara. They want girls aged twelve to fifteen who are dancing on pointe. We'll take you all down for the audition next week."

I look around the room. Edie's biting her lower lip, chin set determinedly. Iako's smiling and hugging herself. Julie is bouncing on her toes. Cam is grinning widely.

We all want it. We wouldn't be here if we didn't. But, of course, most of us will be disappointed. That's the nature of ballet, I guess—only a very few will make it all the way to the top.

It sucks.

I look at Melissa. She is standing very still, her shoulders back and her head held high. She looks every inch a dancer. If I had to guess, right now, I'd say she's got a better shot at Clara than anyone else here.

But I have every intention of dancing my heart out.

* * *

At break, Melissa gathers her group of friends around her. Actually, they all just seem to gravitate to her, like moons orbiting a planet. I follow, because I don't know what else to do and because Edie is grabbing my elbow.

"So," Melissa says, "we need to talk."

"We need to vote," Anya says, giggling.

"Yeah! Who's next, Melissa? No-bun Cam?" Zoe makes a face, showing two rows of braces with blue bands.

Melissa nods. "Definitely."

"Just because of her hair?" I ask. "She's actually really friendly, Melissa. She seems super nice."

"*Nice* isn't the point," Melissa snaps. "*Nice* doesn't make you a dancer."

"She's a good dancer too," I say.

Melissa snorts. "She looks more like a wrestler."

I know what she means. Cam has broad shoulders and an athletic build. She's solid muscle, and although she dances well, she doesn't have the leggy elegance of Iako, Melissa and Mackenzie. "She kicked butt in modern this morning," I say.

"Yeah. In modern," Melissa says. "But ballet? Come on."

Edie nods. "Melissa's right, Cassandra. Cam doesn't really have the body type you need for a career in ballet. Her neck's too short, for one thing. And maybe that's not fair, but that's the way it is."

Across the grass, Cam and the other new girls are standing and talking together. Cam has an arm across Iako's shoulders, and as I watch, she throws her head back and laughs.

"So," Melissa says. "Hands up for voting Cam off."

Without a moment's hesitation, Zoe's, Anya's, Danika's and Edie's hands all fly up.

I hate being a part of this. I hate it.

"Cassandra?" Melissa's voice is cold.

I stand there for a moment, my heart beating fast. I can see my dad's face and I know exactly what he'd say. *Just do what you know is right, Cassie, and everything else will fall into place.*

"Come on, Cassie." Edie nudges me, her forehead creased with worry lines.

"Are you in?" Melissa puts her hands on her hips. "Or out?"

"Out," I say. "I'm out." My stomach is tight, and something is fluttering in my chest. I head back into the school alone and wait outside the studio door for our next class to begin.

A few minutes later I am joined by Cam and the other new girls. Cam is smiling as she does a temps levé in arabesque across the hallway.

If she knew what Melissa and the others were saying about her...I manage to force a grin, despite my anxiety. "What's up?"

"Nothing," she says. "Just looking forward to the next class."

I'd almost forgotten. All this drama with Melissa and Edie...it has actually made me lose sight of what is important: my dancing. "Let's just go in there and dance our hearts out," I say.

Cam holds up a fist, and I bump my knuckles against hers. Over her shoulder, I see Melissa, Edie and the others heading toward us. Melissa's chin is lifted, her gaze straight, and one hand rests on an angled hip. Every line of her body expresses her fury.

* * *

I do my best to push away thoughts about what happened at the break and focus on my dancing. Diana walks around as usual, correcting our positions, lifting our legs higher, reminding us to soften our arms, to keep our shoulders down and back. I don't think I am dancing my best. In fact, I know I'm not. I'm concentrating as hard as I can, and I know my positions are technically correct, but when we all go into the center to dance, I can't feel the music in my body like I usually do. All I can feel is the cold clutch of anxiety in my belly.

If I dance like this at the audition, I won't have a chance of getting the part of Clara. Clara should be playful, lighthearted. Diana tells us to stop and shake it out, and I take a moment to look around at the others and wonder who will be chosen. Much as I hate to admit it, Melissa's dancing is always magical. Almost flawless, though of course Diana can usually find something to criticize in every one of us. Edie isn't as dazzling as Melissa, but she's neat and capable in an all-round way. Mackenzie is good too, and Anya. It's hard to compare, because we all have different weaknesses. Iako is by far the most flexible—when Diana lifted her leg above her head during the barre exercises, it was unbelievable how high she could go—but Diana says she needs to work more on strength. And none of us have the powerful jumps that Cam does.

Finally, class is over. We stretch out our muscles and unlace our shoes. I slip on a hoodie, put my pointe shoes back in my bag and take a drink from my water bottle. My heart is beating fast, and it isn't just from the dancing.

If I can't shake off my fear—or at least keep it from affecting my performance—I won't even need Melissa to sabotage my chances.

Eight

That evening at the Harrisons' is uncomfortable, to say the least. I try to act normal, but it is hard, since Edie is doing her best to avoid talking to me.

"Everything okay, girls?" Mrs. Harrison asks us over dinner.

"Fine," we both say.

"Anything interesting happen today?"

I've just taken a huge bite of my chicken burger, so I can only nod vigorously.

"There're going to be auditions next week, for *The Nutcracker*," Edie says. She drizzles Italian dressing onto her salad. "Our class is going to try out." She puts the bottle down and presses her hands together like she's praying. "I want to be Clara so bad."

Mr. and Mrs. Harrison exchange looks across the dinner table. "Ah," Mrs. Harrison says.

"Probably it'll be one of the new girls," Edie says. "Seems like the teachers are mostly paying attention to them."

"Well, they have to. They don't know them like they know you lot. Besides, I'm sure the school wants to attract new students," Mr. Harrison says. "Can you pass the ketchup, Cassandra?"

I pass him the ketchup. "I haven't noticed that," I say. "Seems to me that they pay plenty of attention to everyone. Besides, I doubt whoever judges the audition will know who's new and who isn't."

Edie snorts rudely, and Mr. and Mrs. Harrison exchange looks again.

Mrs. Harrison leans toward her daughter, her forehead creasing. "Edie, what is it? Did something happen? What's wrong?"

Edie shrugs her off. "Nothing's wrong."

"Edie's used to getting quite a bit of fuss made over her at the school," Mr. Harrison says. "You and Melissa, you're their rising stars, aren't you?"

"Dad!" Edie rolls her eyes. "Please."

He looks at me. "Edie gets jealous sometimes. Only child, you know? It'll be good for her to have you here. She's a bit too used to having the world revolve around her."

My cheeks burn, and I stare at the table's shiny wooden surface, wishing he'd just stop talking. He's making everything a thousand times worse. Edie pushes her chair back, stands up and storms out of the dining room.

Mrs. Harrison gives me an apologetic look. "Well, maybe you two both need some alone time," she says.

So I spend the rest of the evening reading in my room while Edie watches television downstairs. I can't concentrate on my book though. I keep replaying the day in my head—the girls voting Cam off, Melissa's anger when I refused to take part, my lousy dancing in class—and it's hard not to feel a little sorry for myself.

I wish I was home in Australia with my own family.

* * *

Mrs. Harrison drives us back to the academy the next morning. Edie doesn't say much in the car, but as soon as we are out of her mom's earshot, she turns to me. "I can't believe you did that. Why couldn't you just vote Cam off with the rest of us?"

I look at her. "It was mean," I say. "I don't get it. Melissa's an amazing dancer—she doesn't need to be scared of competition."

"She isn't," Edie says. "She just doesn't want to see the teachers making the wrong decisions."

I shrug. "I'm pretty sure they know what they're doing."

"Well, it isn't what you think that matters." Edie's eyes are suddenly shining with tears. "She was willing to let you be part of our group because you're staying with me. And now you've wrecked everything by being so stupid."

"Just because I wouldn't take part in her mean little games?"

"You don't get it." Edie wipes a hand roughly across her eyes. "It isn't a game, Cassandra. Maybe you haven't noticed, but no one's even talking to Iako since the vote."

"I am," I say. "And so are the other new girls."

"Yeah, whatever." She shrugs as if to say that the new girls don't count.

"Don't you think it's kind of mean?" I ask her. "Honestly, Edie?" She isn't meeting my gaze, and I think that deep down she knows it isn't okay. A cluster of girls is standing just ahead of us on the front steps, and I stop walking and lightly touch Edie's arm. "If you didn't go along with it, she couldn't do the stuff she does. Why don't you stand up to her?"

She shakes my hand off. "Because," she says, "Melissa is my best friend. Besides, I'm not stupid."

"What does that mean?" I'm a little annoyed that she's called me stupid twice in about two minutes.

"You'll see," she says and runs off ahead of me into the school.

* * *

Inside, a crowd of girls is jostling in front of the bulletin board.

"It's about the auditions!" Cam calls out when she sees me.

"It is?" I push closer to double-check. Sure enough, there is a flyer posted from the Pacific Coast Ballet, with the times and location for the *Nutcracker* auditions. I turn to look at her.

"Oh my god, Cam. Can you imagine being Clara? I'm not going to be able to think about anything else."

Cam runs her fingers through her hair, making it stick up. "Yeah, tell me about it. I dreamed about *The Nutcracker* last night. Only, in my dream, the Sugar Plum Fairy was chasing Clara around on a broomstick." She shakes her head. "Guess I shouldn't read Harry Potter right before bed."

Melissa's sharp voice speaks up from behind me. "Cam, you're not really expecting to be Clara, are you? I mean, you can't help it, but... well, let's just say you don't really have the body type for ballet."

"I made it here, didn't I?" Cam says. She is shorter than Melissa and tilts her chin up to meet her eyes. "I got accepted for the summer program."

"Cam has the best jumps of any of us," I say.

They both ignore me. They look like two dogs staring each other down, waiting to see who will give way first. To my surprise, it's Melissa who looks away.

"Girls! I realize this is exciting, but I still expect you to be in class on time," Mrs. Hoffman says.

The chatter subsides and we all make our way into the studio for the day's first session, which is jazz—something I love almost as much as ballet. The music is alive inside me, filling me with energy and lightness—motion and emotion. Every part of my body wants to dance.

But my brain won't switch off. I can't stop thinking about the audition. Can I dance well enough to get the part of Clara?

Nine

At lunch, I head outside alone. Edie and Melissa have been ignoring me all morning, and I don't think I'm welcome in their little group anymore. Not that I want to be. They're being totally mean to Cam, making snotty comments about her hair, laughing behind her back. I cross the grass and find a spot to sit, alone, on a bench under the trees.

I need to think. I need to stay focused on why I am here. I close my eyes for a moment and concentrate on the feel of the sun on my face, the sound of the distant traffic, my breath going in and out. My mom went through a meditation phase a year or so ago, and I used to meditate with her, the two of us in *zazen*, as she called it, cross-legged in our living room, listening to some guided visualization she'd downloaded. The guy who led the meditation had a strong accent that Dad liked to imitate. Mom got annoyed at him for it, but he was just trying to make me laugh.

The memory loosens an avalanche of emotion and a homesickness so strong I'm scared I might start bawling. *Focus. Focus. You're here to dance.* I grit my teeth and open my eyes.

Cam is walking toward me. I wave. "Hey."

"You're not with your friends today?" She stops in front of me.

"No. Well, they're not really my friends. It's just that I'm staying with Edie, you know? Her folks are my homestay family."

"Ah." She relaxes a little. "That makes sense. I wondered why you were always with them—I mean, instead of with the other homestay girls."

"Where are you all staying?" I ask, curious.

"I'm staying with some old friends of my parents, actually. Julie and Mackenzie are staying with a family that has two young boys who do ballet. Eight-year-old twins. I think it's pretty crazy over there."

"And Iako?"

"She's staying with an older couple, two women who always take students from Japan. She's helping them learn Japanese, and they help her with her English." She sits down on the bench beside me and opens her lunch bag. "So is it okay for you? I mean, staying with Edie?"

"Yeah. Her parents are nice. I'm just a bit homesick, I guess." My throat closes up on the last words, and I have to look away.

"Aw. Yeah, I have it easy, staying with people I know." She takes an apple out of her bag and crunches into it loudly. "Do you know what's up with Edie and Melissa and their friends? I mean, I get that they don't like me, but the stuff they were saying this morning..."

"I know. That was really mean." I hesitate, wondering whether I should try to explain the whole stupid voting thing. I don't want to admit that I actually took part. I remember my own hand going up to vote against Iako, as if I were nothing more than a puppet with no mind of my own. "Melissa's very competitive," I say.

"Ha. You think?"

I laugh. "I guess that was kind of stating the obvious. But the thing is—well, maybe she feels kind of threatened by the new girls, you know? She really wants to get into PTP."

"Who doesn't?"

"I don't know if I do," I admit. "I mean, I sort of do. But I'd miss my family so much."

To my surprise, Cam doesn't even raise an eyebrow. "PTP's not the only route to being a dancer," she says, and takes another bite of her apple.

"It's kind of hard to remember that when it's all anyone talks about." I open my lunch bag, reach my hand in—and snatch it back out with a shriek. Instead of a plastic-wrapped sandwich, my fingers touched something slimy.

"What's wrong?"

"I don't know." I dump the contents of the bag out onto the grass and stare at the slippery pink mess. "Ugh."

Cam bends closer. "Looks like your yogurt spilled over everything."

"I guess so." I pick up the plastic container. "The lid's still on tight. Weird." My heart sinks. I open the container, but, just as I guessed, there's no yogurt left inside. "Someone dumped it," I say flatly.

"Who would do that?" Cam says.

I just look at her. "Take a guess."

"Melissa? But—well, why on earth would she do that? Messing with your lunch is hardly going to help her dance career."

"She's mad at me," I say. "Because I wouldn't go along with her games."

"What games?"

I take a deep breath. "She's playing this stupid game, like we're all on some reality show or something. She's voting people off."

Cam laughs out loud. "She's doing *what*?"

I guess it is kind of funny. In a way. If you don't think about it too much. "She's deciding who she thinks shouldn't be here," I explain. "And then she gets her friends to vote to get rid of that person."

"Let me guess," Cam says. "They voted for me."

I nod. "I'm sorry."

"Don't apologize," she says grimly. "It's not your fault. I mean, you didn't take part in it, did you?"

I shake my head. "Melissa asked if I was in or out. I said out."

Cam points at my ruined lunch. "And that's why she did this?"

"Yeah. I think so."

"That is seriously messed up," she says.

"Do you think we should tell anyone?" I ask.

Cam looks thoughtful. "Well, she hasn't really done anything except mess up your lunch, and we can't prove that."

"No. I know."

She looks down at her apple, slowly turning it in her hands. "I wonder why they picked me to vote off first."

Cam sounds more curious than hurt, but I hate that she's even thinking about this. "They didn't," I say. "They started with Iako."

"They voted Iako off? Seriously?"

"We all did," I say miserably. "I did too, Cam. I feel horrible about it now."

Cam takes a last bite of her apple, drops the core back into her lunch bag and chews slowly. She doesn't say anything for a while, and I wonder what she's thinking. I can't imagine Cam doing anything just because Melissa told her to. There's nothing puppetlike about her. "Why did you do that?" she asks at last.

"I don't know." I make a face. "I didn't like it, but I figured who cares if the girls are playing games and voting? I told myself that the teachers would see who could dance. It isn't a popularity contest."

"Yeah, but still. You didn't have to vote."

"I wish I hadn't," I say. "I was scared, I guess."

"So what changed? I mean, why didn't you vote for me too?" Her eyes meet mine, direct and challenging.

"I guess I was feeling bad about Iako. And I thought, you know, that we were...well, friends. Sort of."

"We are."

"It wasn't just that," I say. "I'd seen what had happened to Iako, and I was wrong about it not mattering. I mean, it wasn't just the vote. It was what happened afterward. They all stopped talking to her. You can see it totally affecting her confidence. Even her dancing seems kind of flat, you know?"

"She was already homesick anyway," Cam says. "But now that everyone's ignoring her, she's really a mess. She was crying in the girls' bathroom after class this morning." There's an edge of anger in her voice.

"I think they might be doing more than just ignoring her," I say.

"What do you mean?"

I take another deep breath. "I think Melissa took Iako's shoes. Before that first pointe class, remember?

Edie says that Melissa didn't do it, but I don't know if I believe her."

"What about the other girls? Danika and Anya and Zoe?"

I shrug. "They go along with whatever Melissa says."

"Right." Cam frowns, blue eyes narrowing and eyebrows pulling together. I can practically hear the gears turning in her mind. "We can't let them get to us," she says. "I mean, you were right, in a way. It's what the teachers think that matters. They decide who gets invited to stay."

If what Melissa is doing is affecting Iako's dancing, the teachers might not see her potential. "Do you think we should tell Iako? So that she doesn't take it so personally?"

She nods. "And Mackenzie and Julie. They're next, I assume."

"I guess so." A giant fist is squeezing my stomach. "Do we have to tell them about me voting for Iako? It's not that I'm ashamed of it." I shake my head, taking back those words. "I mean, of course I am—I feel awful. But I don't want to hurt her feelings."

"I think she'd understand," Cam says. "But don't worry. I won't say anything."

Ten

Before the lunch break ends, Cam and I find the other new girls sitting together near the entrance steps, and I fill them in on what Melissa and her friends have been doing.

Julie rips off a chunk of her fruit bar and chews ferociously. "What a total bitch."

Mackenzie is sitting in the splits, stretching. Her dark-lashed eyes are huge, her mouth a perfect O. "I can't believe she'd do that," she says at last. "It's so *mean*."

"I don't understand," Iako says.

"Okay," Cam says. "You know those TV shows? Like *Survivor*, or—"

Iako shakes her head. "No, no. I understand this. She voted me off the island. But why? I don't understand why she does this."

"It is horrible," I say. "But maybe it's a compliment, Iako. She's jealous of you."

"Jealous? I'm sorry. I don't understand."

"She thinks you are her competition," I say. "Because you're a good dancer."

"We're all good dancers," she says.

"I know." I look around at the four girls, noting Julie's fury, Mackenzie's wide-eyed indignation, Iako's puzzled frown, Cam's resigned expression. "So here's what I think, okay? Melissa only has as much power as we give her."

Cam nods. "It's what the teachers think that matters. That's who decides who gets invited to stay."

"So we just ignore Melissa, right? We don't let her get to us." Julie looks thoughtful. "Actually, maybe we should really ignore her, like she's doing to Iako. Pretend she doesn't exist."

I shake my head. "No. Then we're as bad as she is. We're not going to play her games."

Mackenzie swings her legs back together. "Got it," she says. "We stay focused and we dance our best." Then she grins. "And we beat her and Edie for the two Claras."

* * *

That evening, Edie's parents take us out for dinner at a fancy Italian restaurant with a fireplace, red-brick walls with dark wood beams, and white tablecloths. Mr. Harrison orders wine for himself and Edie's mom, and Shirley Temples for me and Edie. I've never had one before. It's got different-colored fruit juice floating in layers, and a cherry speared on a plastic skewer.

"We're celebrating," Mrs. Harrison says. "Both of you auditioning for Clara! So exciting."

Mr. Harrison lifts his glass. "A toast! To two beautiful girls and amazing young dancers."

We all clink our glasses together, and my eyes meet Edie's for a second. I wonder what she is thinking. I take a sip of my drink, which is as sweet as honey. "Thank you," I say, dropping my eyes to the menu in front of me.

"Edie's favorite is the spaghetti and meatballs," Mr. Harrison says. "Right, Edie?"

"It used to be," she says. "When I was about ten."

"Sounds good to me," I say. Actually, it sounds great. I'm starving.

We make polite conversation while we eat, but it's strained. I'm sure Edie's parents can tell that things between the two of us are tense. When I get up to use the washroom, Edie follows me.

"We have to talk," she says, leaning against the counter.

"We do?" I raise my eyebrows. "You ignored me all day."

"I know, but it doesn't have to be like this." Her eyes meet mine. "If you would apologize to Melissa—"

I cut her off. "Apologize to her? You're kidding me."

Her cheeks flush. "She's really mad, Cassandra."

"She's the one who should apologize," I say. "To me and Iako and Cam."

"You don't understand."

"I understand plenty," I say. "Melissa's crazy, Edie. Either that or she's just nasty. I don't get why you don't stand up to her."

"She's my best friend," Edie says.

"So be a friend to her, then. Tell her to quit being such a bully." I study Edie's expression, wondering what she's thinking. "She's a good dancer," I say. "She doesn't need to do this stuff."

"I know," Edie says. There's a catch in her voice. "Please tell her you're sorry, Cassandra."

"Not a chance," I say. "The only thing I'm sorry about is not standing up to her earlier."

"I don't know what she's going to do." Her shoulders slump. "And I don't know what she'll make *me* do."

"She can't *make* you do anything," I say a little scornfully. "You don't have to go along with her."

"Yes, I do," Edie says. "I'm not like you and Cam."

"What do you mean?"

"You know. Like, not caring what people think."

"I care," I say, surprised.

She shakes her head. "Maybe. But you didn't vote for Cam, did you? You just said no. I couldn't do that. Melissa would be furious."

"You're scared of her? Some friendship."

"We've been friends since we were ten," Edie says. "There's lots about Melissa that you don't understand."

I walk away from her, heading back out the bathroom door. "That's for sure," I say over my shoulder.

Edie is just standing there, staring at herself in the mirror.

Eleven

The next few days pass uneventfully. We dance all day—ballet, modern, jazz—and I spend my evenings reading, stretching, practicing. Sometimes I talk to Cam on the phone, or I borrow Edie's computer and check Facebook or email my friends back home. The audition is getting closer, and although the divide between the new girls and Melissa's gang is as obvious as ever, nothing awful has happened.

I start to relax a little. I start to think that maybe Melissa has given up on her scheming.

And then the poop hits the fan.

When Edie and I arrive at school on Friday morning, Diana confronts me in the hallway. "Cassandra, come with me to the office, please."

"What is it?" I ask. "Is something wrong?"

"Just come with me." Diana's face is grim, her lips set in a thin, straight line.

I turn to Edie, but she won't look at me. "What's wrong?" I ask again, quickening my steps to keep up with Diana as she marches down the hall.

"I think you know," she says curtly.

"But I don't!" Her coldness—and the unexpectedness of it—feels like a slap to the face. My eyes are stinging, and I have to blink away tears. "I haven't done anything."

She opens the office door and steps back to let me go in ahead of her. Mrs. Hoffman is already there, sitting stiff and straight-backed behind a desk. She gestures for me to take a seat on a couch across from her, and I sink into it, feeling small and scared. Diana perches on the arm of the couch as if she doesn't want to be any closer to me than she has to.

"What is going on?" I ask. My heart is racing.

Mrs. Hoffman takes off her reading glasses and lets them dangle around her neck. Then she turns her laptop around to face me. I lean forward, confused, and start reading what's on the screen.

I recognize the image immediately. "The school's Facebook page?" I say, puzzled. Then I look more closely at where Mrs. Hoffman's finger is pointing. There's a post from the ballet school: *Congratulations to our dancers who are auditioning for The Nutcracker! Good luck to you all!*

And underneath it, in the comments, is my name. My face. And a comment—apparently my comment: *Ya, cuz they're gonna need it! especially Miss floppy-foot Edie and spaghetti-arms Melissa!! lmao!!*

The air rushes out of my lungs in a whoosh. I can't catch my breath. "I...that wasn't...I didn't..." I can barely form the words in my mouth. Mrs. Hoffman and Diana are both looking at me, their faces grave. "I didn't write that," I say. "I wouldn't ever say that." For a second, it seems so absurd that it's almost funny. I can't believe anyone would think I'd write that.

"There's nothing to smile about," Mrs. Hoffman says coldly.

"I'm not—I just—it's so ridiculous! You can't really believe I'd write that."

Diana and Mrs. Hoffman exchange glances and say nothing, and a panicky feeling starts to build in my chest.

"Honestly," I say. "It wasn't me. I swear."

"How do you think this happened, then?" Diana asks, and her voice is surprisingly gentle.

"I don't know," I say. "No one knows my password, so I don't see...unless..."

"Unless?" She leans closer to me. "Unless what, Cassandra?"

I'm remembering last night. I borrowed Edie's computer, tried unsuccessfully to Skype my folks, emailed a friend, checked Facebook. Did I log out? I can't remember. Would Edie have posted as me, deliberately, to get me in trouble?

I don't want to believe it.

"I don't know," I say. "But I know I didn't post that comment. So I don't know how—but someone else must have done it." I can't decide if I should mention Edie or not. I remember her following me to the restaurant bathroom, trying to get me to apologize to Melissa. *I don't know what she'll make me do,* she said.

I don't see how anyone other than Edie could have done this—but I don't know for sure, and I don't want to accuse her if there's even a small chance that I'm wrong.

"Cassandra, please tell the truth," Mrs. Hoffman puts in. "People make mistakes, but lying only makes matters worse."

I start to cry—I can't help it. "I'm not lying," I say. "I think I must have forgotten to sign out of Facebook and—well, someone else—posted in my name." Even as I say it, I know how unlikely it must sound.

The two of them exchange glances again.

"I personally think we should withdraw her from the audition," Mrs. Hoffman says. "At the very least."

"No, please," I say. I wipe the tears from my eyes and try to steady my voice. "I don't know how this happened, but I swear I didn't post that comment. I don't even think that way."

Diana looks thoughtful. "I must admit I was surprised when I saw this." She looks at Mrs. Hoffman. "Cassandra has always seemed supportive of other girls in class."

"It is very disappointing behavior," Mrs. Hoffman says.

Diana nods. "Yes, it is. Inexcusable behavior."

Mrs. Hoffman sighs heavily. "We'll have to discuss this further and decide on an appropriate consequence," she says. "In the meantime, I'd suggest that you delete that comment."

My face burning, I sign in to Facebook, delete the awful words beside my name and log out again. "I hope no one else has seen it," I say.

"So do I," Diana says. "I suspect you'll find out soon enough." She stands up. "Go ahead. You'd better get to class. I'll be there shortly."

Twelve

I walk through the door and into the dance studio and instantly the movement and chatter stops dead. Nine girls freeze mid-stretch, mid-sentence, mid-laugh. Nine faces turn toward me. Nine pairs of eyes study my face. The silence hangs in the air like a thick fog. I look at Edie, but she drops her eyes. Beside her, Melissa smirks, eyes hard and challenging. My cheeks are ablaze and I feel a sick rush of shame, as if I really have done something horrible. I lift my chin, refusing to give her the satisfaction of seeing how upset I am, and walk through the figures like they are statues—this one in the splits, that one lacing a shoe, this one stretching her hamstrings. Gradually they all resume their movement, and I take a spot in the middle of the room, near Cam and Mackenzie. I sit down and take my shoes out of my bag.

"Cassandra," Cam whispers, "everyone's saying you posted something on Facebook. I haven't seen it, but..." She trails off.

"I saw it," Mackenzie says. "The school posted good luck to the girls who were auditioning—and you said we were going to need it."

At least they're still talking to me. "I didn't post it," I say, too quickly.

Cam looks relieved. "Good. It didn't seem like something you'd say. But then...well, who did?"

"Edie, maybe," I say. "I might've left my Facebook page open on her laptop." I turn to Mackenzie. "I'd never do anything like that. I hope you didn't believe it."

She shrugs, looking uncomfortable. "Well, I didn't know what to think." She doesn't meet my eyes, and I suspect she still isn't convinced.

"Diana and Mrs. Hoffman are talking about not letting me audition," I say.

"That's probably exactly what Edie and Melissa hoped would happen," Cam says. "Mackenzie, you'd better be careful between now and the audition next Thursday. You'll be next, you know."

Mackenzie looks at Cam and me, her Bambi eyes wide and hurt. "You think they don't like me?"

Cam snorts. "Where've you been, Mackenzie? It's got nothing to do with liking you. You're auditioning for Clara, right? You're Melissa's competition."

"What do you think she'll do to me?" she whispers.

"I don't know," I say. "But if I were you, I'd watch your back."

Cam nods. "Yeah, just stay well away from her. And don't leave your bag out of your sight."

"Or your shoes," I say, thinking of Iako.

"Or your lunch," Cam adds.

"Or your laptop, or your phone—" I break off as Diana enters the studio.

"Yeah, okay. I got it." Mackenzie finishes tying her shoes and we all take our positions at the barre. I'm near the front of the line, and I can feel the eyes of the other girls on me. I wonder how many of them think I posted that comment. In my mind, I can't stop replaying the conversation with Diana and Mrs. Hoffman, can't stop thinking of things I should have said, can't stop defending myself.

I remember what Cam and I told the other homestay girls: *Melissa only has as much power as we give her. It's what the teachers think that matters.*

I've underestimated Melissa. She is well aware that the teachers have the final say in who will be asked to stay on in the fall.

And now, thanks to her and Edie, the teachers think I am an unprofessional, badly behaved, spoiled brat.

"First position," Diana says curtly, skipping her usual words of welcome. "No talking, please. I expect to see some good effort from you all today."

"Yes, Diana," we chorus.

At the barre, I do my best to tune out the other girls. Instead, I find myself thinking about my parents. They wouldn't believe for one single second that I'd make that awful comment. They know I'm not like that. Peter knows it too, and so do all my friends back home, even the ones who don't understand why I care so much about dancing. They all believe in me, no matter what.

Again, my dad's words come back to me. *Just do what you know is right, Cassie.* I imagine my anger and anxiety as a red-hot ball of energy, and I channel it into my dancing, straining for better turnout and higher lifts, stretching every muscle to the limit.

Pliés. Relevés. Développés. Retirés.

I want so badly to show Diana—to show everyone—that I'm not the kind of person who would stoop to posting nasty comments online. I think about what Diana said in our first class, about dance being the hidden language of the soul. I wish she could see the truth in my dancing. I wish I could dance so beautifully that everyone watching would know that I don't have that kind of anger or jealousy or spitefulness inside me.

I dig deeper than ever, ignoring the fatigue in my muscles, tuning out the pain as I push myself to my limit and beyond. *I will be a dancer,* I whisper under my breath. *I will be a dancer, no matter what. Focus. Focus. Breathe.*

"Very nice, Cassandra," Diana says as she passes me. Her hand touches my shoulder briefly, pushing it down and back, and my eyes meet hers. "Well done."

I mumble, "Thank you," and she continues on down the line.

Did she see? I watch her walk away and find myself holding my breath, hoping. Could she see what I was trying to show her?

* * *

Cam and Mackenzie stand by me, but the rest of the girls cut me dead, ignoring me completely or, worse, making sharp little comments under their breath as I walk past. Even Julie and Iako turn away when they see me. The story seems to have spread beyond our class—girls I don't even know stare at me in the halls, give me dirty looks, whisper to each other and giggle. Maybe they saw the comment on Facebook before I deleted it. More likely, Melissa has done her best to spread the story.

It isn't until it's time to go home that I think of the Harrisons. My stomach knots and my mouth suddenly tastes sour. Will Edie tell them? And will they believe that I posted that comment?

Thirteen

Mrs. Harrison picks us up as usual, and she's smiling. "Good day?"

I guess she doesn't know. "All right," I say.

Edie shrugs and gets into the passenger seat beside her mother. I hold my breath, waiting, but she doesn't say anything.

Which doesn't mean she won't. I can't relax yet.

"I thought we'd get a movie this evening," Mrs. Harrison says. "Friday night! I bet your bodies will be glad of a little rest this weekend."

In the back seat, I buckle my seat belt. "Definitely," I say. My legs feel as weak as a toddler's and my left hip hurts, and my toes—well, I don't even want to think about my toes.

"Can Melissa come over?" Edie says. "And can we get that ballet movie? The new one, that documentary?"

"What a nice idea," her mother says.

I didn't think things could get worse, but they just did. I can't imagine spending the evening with Edie and Melissa.

Maybe I'll pretend to be sick and just go to bed.

* * *

When we get back to the house, I head up to my room. I change into my old flannel pants and a black long-sleeved T-shirt, and I curl up on my bed. I ache all over, and it's not just my muscles. I want to cry, but I'm too exhausted. If a fairy godmother appeared right now and offered to wave her wand and send me home, I'd be gone.

I can't imagine how I'm going to get through two more weeks of this.

I push my face into the pillow. It's pale blue, silky and cool and smells like fabric softener. I think of my own well-worn red-plaid pillowcase and a wave of homesickness rushes over me. I think about calling my parents, but there's the time difference, and I'd have to borrow Edie's computer. And I don't know why, but I feel oddly ashamed, like I've done something wrong. I don't want my parents to know about the Facebook comment beside my name.

Then there's a knock and my bedroom door opens.

I sit up. It's Mrs. Harrison. She steps into my room and closes the door behind her, and I see her creased forehead and the hard line of her mouth.

My heart gives a jolting kick high in my chest.

She knows.

"Cassandra," she says, "I just heard something extremely disturbing. Something about you posting a very hurtful comment on Facebook."

I shake my head. "I didn't, Mrs. Harrison. I know what it said, but I wouldn't ever do that."

She frowns, her plucked and penciled eyebrows moving toward each other like two skinny black worms. "Then how do you suggest that this happened? The comment was in your name."

I can hardly tell her that her own daughter must have done it. "Someone must have signed in as me," I say. "Maybe I forgot to sign out of my account."

"I hope you aren't trying to shift the blame to Edie," she says sharply. "She's been very loyal, you know. She didn't even tell me what you did. I only heard just now, from Melissa's mother. She called to let me know. Apparently Melissa is very upset."

I'm pretty sure the whole thing was Melissa's idea. "I'm not trying to blame anyone," I say. "I just know I didn't do it."

"This Facebook business, all this cyberbullying...I've read about it happening, but really, Cassandra, I wouldn't have thought you would do anything like this." She leans toward me, tilts her head and tries to look me in the eye. "Is there something going on that you'd like to talk about? If you're having a hard time making friends with the other girls or feeling homesick...well, I hope you'd tell me."

I don't say anything, because what else can I say? I can't make her believe me.

She sighs. "Well, I can't make you talk about it."

The lump in my throat is so huge, I don't think I could say anything even if I wanted to.

"I don't want you using the computer this weekend," Mrs. Harrison says. "Obviously it's a privilege you can't be trusted with."

I swallow. That means no email, no Skype, no contact with my friends or my parents.

"Melissa will be here soon," she says. "I hope you'll apologize to her and Edie." She sighs again. "You can't take back what you have said, but you need to figure out how you are going to repair the damage you have done. It's up to you to make things right with them."

I clench my hands into tight fists, nails digging into my palms. "I'll talk to them," I say. The words come out hard as pellets and leave a bitter taste in my mouth.

"Good," Mrs. Harrison says. She turns to leave but not without a parting shot. "If it were up to me, you would lose the privilege of auditioning next week," she says. "Edie started to cry when I told her that, just so you know. She doesn't want that to happen. Personally, I think she is being far more generous than you deserve."

The unfairness of it all is feeding the growing fury inside me, and I'm scared of what might come out if I try to answer.

She takes my silence for stubbornness, or perhaps heartless indifference, and makes a little noise of disgust before walking away and closing my bedroom door much harder than necessary.

I sit motionless on the bed for a long time, just breathing deeply and trying to calm myself. I feel like screaming, or crying, but there's no point.

I need a plan.

I need to stand up to Melissa and Edie somehow. I can't let them win.

I get off the bed and look at myself in the full-length mirror. First position. Second. Third. Chin up, back straight, shoulders down and back, turn out from the hip...Despite everything, I danced better today than I ever have. I know I did. And I can see the dancer in the mirror, looking back at me with determination in every line of her body.

Courage. Passion. Dedication. This is how I will beat Melissa and Edie. I will apologize if I must, lying through my teeth, and I will not let them see that it hurts. And I will go back to the school on Monday and convince Diana to let me audition.

I will dance my heart out.

I will get the part of Clara, and that will be my revenge.

* * *

When Melissa arrives, I go downstairs and join her and Edie in the living room.

She looks at me, eyebrows lifted, mouth curled into a smirk. Edie looks down and tugs at a loose thread in the cuff of her hoodie.

I take a deep breath. "That comment on Facebook was awful," I say. "It was a mean thing to write. And it was a lie, anyway." I meet Melissa's eyes and hope she knows exactly what I am really saying: *You're mean. You're a liar.*

"I just figured you were jealous," she says. "Because, you know, Edie and I probably have a better chance than you do of being Clara."

I force a smile. "Probably," I say. "I guess we'll all have to wait and see."

Mrs. Harrison is standing in the doorway between the kitchen and the living room, listening and nodding approvingly at our civilized behavior. If only she knew...

"Well, may the best dancer win," Melissa says.

* * *

I get through the weekend somehow. Mrs. Harrison is cool toward me, but Mr. Harrison seems to think the whole thing is rather funny. "Girls and their drama," he says. I bet he wouldn't be laughing if he knew the truth.

When I'm alone with Edie on Saturday, I ask her directly if she posted the comment. She doesn't answer, but she can't meet my eyes. "Just tell me the truth," I say. "It's not like anyone's going to believe me anyway. Besides, I already know you did it. You're the only one who could have got into my account."

"Why ask, then?" she says.

"I want to hear you admit it," I say.

Her cheeks are red and her eyes are too bright. "So what if I did?" she says. Her voice is high and shaky, like she's on the edge of tears. "What are you going to do about it?"

"I'm just going to dance," I say.

* * *

On Monday morning, Diana pulls me aside. "We're going to let you go ahead with the audition for *The Nutcracker*," she says. "But I should warn you, Cassandra. Any more incidents like the one last week, and the consequences will be severe."

My heart leaps and flutters like a dancer doing entrechats inside my rib cage. "Thank you," I whisper.

She nods, hesitates as if she is going to say something and then shakes her head. "I'll see you in class."

I watch her go. I want her to believe me. I hate that people are thinking badly of me.

Getting the part of Clara might be a good way to get even with Melissa and Edie, but it won't erase the dark mark against me. It won't clear my name.

And I'm starting to realize that might be more important to me than revenge.

Fourteen

Mackenzie is jumpy all week, figuring that she'll be the next girl voted off, but nothing else happens. We're all worked half to death in every class, so maybe Melissa and the other girls just haven't had the energy for their usual games.

And finally, Thursday—audition day—arrives.

The auditions are being held at a dance studio downtown. It's a bit of a zoo when we first arrive, because the youngest kids are just leaving. There are dozens of them, cute little munchkins, maybe six or seven years old, all chattering nonstop as their parents herd them up and usher them out the door. I watch their excited faces and wonder which ones will end up onstage—they'll be the mice, I guess, and they'll never forget it.

We gather in a wide hallway, and someone hands out our numbers. I get number thirteen—which is fine, as I've never been superstitious. I pin it to my leotard and look around to see who got number one. Not Melissa, anyway—she's got seventeen pinned to her chest.

"They're just auditioning the party girls now," Diana says. "It'll be half an hour or so before they start calling you in, so try to relax. Do some stretching, get ready, don't stress. And keep the volume down, please!"

The floor is littered with shoes, water bottles, bits of lamb's wool, and I can hear faint piano music drifting from the closed studio door. I find a spot to sit and stretch. Cam sinks down into the splits beside me. "Nervous?"

"Yeah." I'm looking around, checking out the competition. Clusters of girls—all slim, long-limbed, smooth-haired—stand around talking, stretching, fixing their hair, adjusting their numbers. They all seem disturbingly confident, like they've done this a hundred times before. A handful of adults is bustling about, making sure each girl is numbered and counted and where she should be. "There sure are a lot of people trying out, aren't there?" I say quietly.

"No kidding." Cam leans forward, chin almost to the floor. "I'd sort of forgotten that there are so many other ballet schools here."

"Odds are, Clara won't even be someone from our school," I say.

Cam sits up. "Not all the schools are as good as the academy."

"I'm going to try not to think about it," I say. "It makes me nervous. I'm just going to dance, and what happens, happens." I slip on my pointe shoes and kneel to lace them, the way Peter taught me. If you kneel on one leg while you lace the other shoe, it's easier to get the tension around your ankle just right.

"You'll do fine," Cam says.

Mackenzie comes and sits down beside us, her back against the wall. "I think I'm going to throw up."

"I know," I say. "Me too."

"Maybe we should both throw up," Mackenzie says glumly. "Gross everyone out so much that they can't dance. Then you and me could get the part."

I laugh. "The Puking Claras. Sounds like a really bad band name."

She laughs, then turns serious. "I don't have a shot anyway."

"Sure you do," I say. "I think you have a better shot than most of us."

"How many black Claras do you think there have been?"

I'm stunned into silence for a moment. It had never occurred to me to wonder. I want to reassure her that of course it doesn't matter—but I have no idea if this is true. I mean, it shouldn't matter. But that doesn't mean anything. "I don't know," I say at last.

"I've seen *The Nutcracker* about a dozen times," she says. "And Clara is always white. Always."

"Well, maybe not this time," I say. "You'd be an awesome Clara."

"Thanks." She sighs, then laughs. "I wish we could tell Andrew Kingsley that Melissa is an evil cow who doesn't deserve an audition, let alone a part in *The Nutcracker*."

"I have to beat her," I say. "And Edie too. I have to."

She stops laughing. “Yeah, you do. You really do.”

“I will,” I say. And I have a sudden rush of confidence. I can do this. I know I can. “Come on,” I say. “Let’s get warmed up.”

* * *

A few minutes later, the studio door opens, hordes of nine- and ten-year-olds—the party girls, I guess—come pouring out and we are called in.

A four-person panel is sitting at the front of the room. One of them—a tall lean man—stands up and introduces himself as Andrew Kingsley. He explains the audition process and tells us what he is looking for. “Clara should be playful,” he says. “Lighthearted, smiling—can you do that?”

We all nod. I glance at my reflection in the mirror and realize my expression is the opposite of lighthearted. More like life or death. I fix a smile on my lips and see the other girls doing the same—which makes me smile for real.

We start out by doing some floor exercises: tendus, pliés, jumps. I feel good—strong, steady, light on my feet. The pianist plays, and we do pirouettes, arabesques, changements. Then we all gather in one corner to do cross-floor exercises. Andrew explains what he wants us to do—one at a time, we are to cross the room diagonally, doing a series of movements. "This will allow us to get a better sense of your abilities," he says. "So you'll go one at a time, and we'll watch each of you as an individual."

This is it, I think. *My chance to show the panel what I can do.* I take a deep breath, trying to slow my racing heart and quiet the chatter in my mind, and listen to what Andrew is asking us to do: temps levé in arabesque, temps levé in retiré, chassé, pas de bourrée.

"Have a large step on the temps levé in arabesque," he says. "Turn out your downstage foot on the chassé, and turn out your trailing foot on the pas de bourrée when you close it into fifth position." Then he smiles. "And show me what the music sounds like," he says. "Joyful. Playful. All right?"

I watch Danika go first, light and graceful, and then Edie. I can feel the music moving through me. Everything is coming together perfectly.

I can do this. I know I can. I step forward, ready to take my turn—

Then something hits my shoulder and spins me around, and I fall, twisting to one side, and land heavily, hitting the floor with my knee, chest, chin. White-hot pain explodes from my ankle and shoots up my leg, and I roll onto my side, clutching my foot between my hands. A wave of nausea rolls over me, and I gasp for breath.

"Oh my god! Are you okay?" Mackenzie's face floats in front of me, wide-eyed and worried. "Can I help you up?"

I can hear myself groaning, making these awful grunting sounds, and I grit my teeth, trying to be quiet, trying not to cry. It hurts so much. Mackenzie reaches out and rubs my back, and I flinch, not wanting to be touched. "My ankle," I say. My face is wet with tears.

"You sort of rolled sideways on it," Mackenzie says. "It looked awful."

Diana's face appears beside hers. "Cassandra? What on earth happened?"

"It's her ankle," Mackenzie says.

"Can you get up?" Diana asks.

I look past her and see all the girls standing still, shocked looks on their faces. The pianist has stopped playing. Andrew Kingsley walks toward us, his forehead creased with concern. When he speaks, he's all business. "Will she be able to continue with the audition?" I hear him ask Diana.

"Yes," I say grimly, even though he wasn't talking to me. "I'm not quitting." With Mackenzie and Diana on either side of me, I try to stand. As soon as my left foot touches the ground, I gasp and clutch Mackenzie's shoulder for support. The pain is excruciating.

Diana shakes her head. "I'm sorry, Cassandra. I think you're going to have to take it easy. Mackenzie, help me get her to a chair."

I hobble and hop to a wooden chair and collapse on it. "May I look?" Diana says.

"Yeah, but don't touch it—" It's all I can do to keep from screaming as she gently unlaces my shoe.

"It's already swelling," she says, her voice low. "You're staying with the Harrisons, aren't you?"

"Yeah." I feel like everything is crashing down around me. I won't be Clara. Worse—what if I've broken my ankle? What if it doesn't heal well enough for me to be a dancer? It's too much—the pain, the disappointment, the dread—and I can't hold back my tears.

Diana turns to the other girls. "Edie, can you please run down to the office and ask the receptionist to call your mother? Cassandra's going to need to get this ankle x-rayed."

Edie's eyes are huge, and her face is pale. She doesn't move from the spot.

"Edie," Diana says sharply. "Now, please."

"Okay," Edie says. She rushes out of the room, and I think she is crying. I can't imagine why—I would have thought she'd be pleased to have me out of the running for Clara.

Maybe even out of the running for PTP. I shove the thought away and look down at my ankle. It's weirdly puffy-looking. It doesn't look like my ankle at all. Somehow that makes me cry even more.

* * *

Edie returns, bringing an ice pack and saying her mom is on her way. The audition goes on without me. Diana asks if I would prefer to wait in the office, but I say I'd rather watch. At least it's a distraction from my ankle, which is throbbing and hurting so much it is making me nauseous.

Mackenzie looks good. So does Melissa, unfortunately. There are a couple of girls I don't know—older girls—who are amazing dancers. Edie, to my surprise, is dancing badly. Her face is flushed and blotchy, and there's nothing playful or light about her dancing.

I can't believe I'm sitting here, watching. Missing the audition. How could I have been so clumsy?

A few minutes later, Mrs. Harrison arrives.

"You poor thing," she says. "We'll make sure you get taken care of properly, don't you worry." She helps me to the car—I sit in the back so I can have my foot up on the seat—and heads to the hospital.

"Thanks for coming to get me," I say.

"Well, of course," she says. Now that I'm hurt, it's like she's forgotten how mad she was at me. "Hopefully they won't make you wait for hours in the emergency room," she says.

"Yeah," I say. I can't stop looking at my ankle. It's fatter and lumpier than ever. It looks like someone else's foot got attached to my leg. Gross. Through the thin pale-pink tights, the skin looks faintly bluish and bruised.

"What happened?" Mrs. Harrison says. "Did you just lose your balance?"

"I don't know," I say. "I think someone bumped into me, but I didn't really see."

"No one else was hurt though?"

"I don't think so," I say. "Everyone kept dancing. And no one said anything." I think back again, remembering. That sudden shove from behind, knocking me off balance, spinning me around...

Did someone push me?

* * *

At the hospital, Mrs. Harrison talks to a nurse and shows her my health-insurance information, and I am helped into a wheelchair. I feel silly, sitting in the emergency room in a ballet leotard, tights and one shoe. I unpin the number from my chest. Thirteen—so much for not being superstitious.

After a few minutes, a doctor looks at my ankle, flexes it a little, which makes me gasp, and asks me if I can curl my toes. "What were you doing, trying to fly?" he says. "Even ballerinas have their limitations."

I don't bother answering.

"Well, it looks to me like it's probably a bad sprain, but we'll take a few pictures and make sure there isn't a fracture." He's short and plump and balding, and he pats my cheek in a way that reminds me a little of my grandfather. "And we'll give you some painkillers. That should cheer you up a little."

"Would a sprain swell up like that?" Mrs. Harrison asks.

"Sure. There's probably some soft-tissue injury, which can cause a lot of swelling." He looks at me. "No dancing for you for a while."

"Even if it's not broken?" I ask.

"A bad sprain can take weeks to heal," he says. "But let's get those X-rays done. If there's a fracture, it could be considerably longer."

My heart sinks. The Summer Intensive is only four weeks altogether, and we're already two weeks into it.

If a few weeks is the best-case scenario, that's it for me.

Game over.

And I've lost.

* * *

I'm wheeled to the X-ray department and helped onto a table, and a heavy lead apron is spread over my body. The technician makes me hold my leg one way and then another, and helps me back into my wheelchair afterward. Mrs. Harrison brings me a hot chocolate from the cafeteria, and we wait to see what the radiologist has to say.

It takes a while, but eventually a tall black woman arrives and introduces herself as Dr. Gentle, which makes me laugh.

"Good name for a doctor," I say.

"Could be worse," she agrees. "I used to work with someone called Dr. Payne."

"Ouch."

"Indeed." She is wearing dark brownish-purple lipstick, and when she smiles, her teeth look startlingly white. "Well, I've got good news and good news. Which do you want first?"

"I'll take the good news," I say.

"Nothing's broken," she says.

"Okay." I know this is good, but right now it is hard to feel happy about it.

"And the other good news?" Mrs. Harrison asks.

"We'll bandage you up, give you some drugs and let you go home." She pats my shoulder. "It'll be pretty sore for a few days, but it should mend just fine. You'll be back on your toes by the end of the summer."

I nod, swallow, taste the salt of my tears on the back of my tongue. "Thanks," I say.

No Clara. No PTP.

The end of the summer will be too late.

Fifteen

Mrs. Harrison drives me home and gets me settled on the couch with my foot up, the TV remote in my hand and a mug of mint tea on the end table beside me. "Now, are you sure you're okay here on your own for a bit? I have to pick up Edie."

"I'll be fine," I say. I'm wondering what is going to happen. I can't just stay here sitting on the couch for the next two weeks. Edie's parents both work. I wonder if they'll send me home or if I'll be able to go to the school and at least watch the classes.

I doubt it, somehow. After that awful Facebook thing, the school will probably be glad to get rid of me.

I flick through the channels, but I can't concentrate on anything, especially not stupid reality-TV shows. My ankle aches and it's all I can do not to cry. To come all this way and have it end with a sprained ankle and everyone hating me...

Eventually I hear the front door open and close, and Edie and Mrs. Harrison walk into the living room. "Cassandra?" Mrs. Harrison says.

I look up. Her expression is serious, and beside her, Edie is red-eyed and teary.

"What's wrong?" I say. "You didn't get the part? Did you find out already? Who got it?"

"Edie has something to say to you." Mrs. Harrison nudges her daughter.

"Sorry," Edie mumbles.

"What for?" For a second, I wonder if she pushed me. But no, she went ahead of me—I was watching her dance when I fell.

"The Facebook comment," Edie mumbles. "I wrote it."

"I know," I say. "You were the only one who could have done it."

She nods. "I told my mom," she says. "And she says I have to tell Diana and Mrs. Hoffman."

I remember the way the two ballet teachers looked at me, so disappointed, that day in the office.

The sense of shame that has followed me like a heavy gray cloud ever since dissipates like fog in the sunshine. "Good," I say. Then I feel a flicker of compassion for Edie. It'll be awful for her, having to admit this to them.

"I'm very sorry too," Mrs. Harrison says. "I'm sorry I didn't believe you, Cassandra."

"It's okay," I say. I can afford to be generous now. "I guess it makes sense that you'd have to believe your own kid."

Her cheeks are flushed almost as pink as Edie's. "She says Melissa told her to do it, but obviously Edie is responsible for her own actions. It doesn't matter whose idea it was."

"Melissa's hard to say no to," I say, and Edie flashes me a grateful glance from beneath wet eyelashes. "Why'd you decide to tell your mom the truth?" I ask her. "I mean, you got away with it. And now you're going to have to tell the teachers and everything."

She shrugs. "Because you got hurt, I guess. And...well, sometimes Melissa scares me. I think she'd do anything to win, you know? She said that if I got the part of Clara and she didn't, she wouldn't even be my friend anymore."

"So who got the part of Clara?" I ask her.

"We don't know yet," she says. "They'll tell us tomorrow, maybe. But it won't be me. I totally blew it."

"Well, it won't be me either." I make a face. "It'll suck if Melissa gets it."

Edie sniffs and rubs her eyes with her knuckles. "She pushed you, didn't she?"

"I don't know," I admit. "I wondered...but I didn't see."

Mrs. Harrison puts her hand on Edie's shoulder. "That's a pretty serious accusation, Edie."

"She said she was going to make sure she got the part," Edie whispers. "She was really upset that the teachers let Cassandra audition—you know, after the Facebook thing."

"That doesn't prove Melissa pushed her," Mrs. Harrison says. "If you don't know for sure, maybe you should keep that suspicion to yourself."

"I won't say anything," I say.

Edie doesn't speak. Her face is blotchy from crying, but her jaw is set stubbornly.

"Edie?" her mother says.

"Melissa pushed her," Edie says. "I know she did."

I don't know if Melissa pushed me or not, but I know one thing: She's pushed Edie too far. And I think that might have been a really big mistake.

* * *

Before I go to bed that night, I call home on Skype. It's early afternoon in Adelaide, so my dad's at work, but my mom's there.

"Cassie! How are you, sweetie?"

"Um, not so good," I say. I fight to hold back tears. "I hurt my ankle."

"Oh honey. Is it bad?"

"Not broken," I say. "I had to get X-rays."

"Oh honey," she says again. She leans in to the camera, like she's trying to get closer to me. "How awful. Can you still dance? Or do you have to rest it?"

"Yeah," I say. "Rest it."

There's a long pause. "Do you want to come home? Because we can change your flight. If you can't dance anyway, maybe you should come home."

I don't answer right away. I imagine being snuggled up cozy on the living room couch with my cat and my mom's quilts and the radio playing, and I think about how homesick I have felt since I got here. I think about Melissa and Edie, and how awful they've been. I think about the Facebook thing and about Diana and Mrs. Hoffman and the Harrisons all looking at me like I was the lowest of the low. Like I was such a disappointment to them all.

I think about how I felt like I was going to cry all the time.

My mom just watches me, waiting. "It's up to you," she says.

Cam stood by me though. She believed in me. And now Edie's admitted what she did, and tomorrow the teachers will know the truth. My name will be cleared, and that ugly black mark will be rubbed away.

Maybe I can't dance right now, but I still don't want to quit.

"I'll stay," I tell her.

She just smiles. "I figured."

* * *

The next day—Friday—my ankle is really sore. I hardly slept , because every time I rolled over, the pain woke me up. I take two painkillers and decide to persuade Mrs. Harrison to take me to the academy with Edie anyway.

"I can still learn stuff by watching," I point out at breakfast. "Oops. Sorry, I just spilled some..." I'm trying to pour milk onto my cereal while balancing on the crutches we borrowed from the hospital.

"Here, let me help." She takes the bowl from me and puts it on the kitchen table. "Are you quite sure you wouldn't rather just take it easy?"

I hop over to my seat. "Yeah. It'll be a distraction."

"I'm so sorry I can't take the day off," Mrs. Harrison says. "It's just that I have these meetings all morning that have taken weeks to arrange."

Edie pours me a glass of orange juice. "She said she wants to watch the classes, Mom."

"It's fine," I say. "Edie's right. I don't want to miss the classes."

Mrs. Harrison takes a last sip of her coffee and puts the mug down on the kitchen counter. "Edie's always saying a dancer has to have courage, passion and dedication." She smiles at me. "I'd say you have all three."

Sixteen

"Are you okay? You look like you're about to throw up," I whisper to Edie as we enter the school. I'm hopping along on my crutches, the impact of every step triggering a throbbing ache in my bandaged ankle, but Edie's moving even more slowly than I am. I stand still for a moment, resting, and let her catch up.

She nods, then changes her mind and shakes her head. "Just nervous about talking to Diana. You know, about the Facebook thing."

"Yeah." I look away. It seems a bit insensitive to let her see how happy I am about this when I know how awful it will be for her. I guess I should be mad at her, but at this point I actually feel kind of sorry for her. "Are you going to tell them it was Melissa's idea?"

"I haven't decided," she says. "I don't want it to look like I'm trying to blame someone else. I mean, I was the one who did it."

"Yeah. But still." It doesn't seem right that Melissa will get away with everything she's done.

Edie's eyes are pink-rimmed. "I'll see you in class," she says.

I watch her walk down the hall to the office. Then I turn and hobble slowly toward the studio to watch the first class. It feels weird to be here wearing jeans and a hoodie instead of my usual leotard and tights.

Mackenzie grabs the door and holds it open for me. "Oh my god, Cassandra! Is it broken?" Her eyes are wide and worried.

"No, just sprained." I collapse onto a low wooden bench along the wall. "Thanks for your help. How'd the rest of the auditions go?"

"Um, okay, I think. We'll probably find out today." She sits down beside me. "I was dreaming about *The Nutcracker* all night. Crazy dreams. The Sugar Plum Fairy turned into a cat and started chasing all the mice."

I laugh. "Cam dreamed the Sugar Plum Fairy was riding a broomstick and chasing Clara."

I turn sideways to put my leg up on the bench. My ankle is still swollen, and I'm supposed to keep it elevated as much as I can.

"When can you dance again?" Mackenzie asks me.

I make a face. "Not soon enough. There's only two weeks left of Summer Intensive—and the doctor said it'll be at least that long before I can walk properly, let alone dance."

She groans. "Seriously? That's awful."

The door opens, and Danika, Anya and Zoe come in, followed by Cam and Iako and, minutes later, Julie and Melissa. Everyone except Edie. I wonder how she's doing, down in the office. I'm surprised how sorry I feel for her.

"Did you see what happened?" I ask Mackenzie in a low voice. "When I fell?"

She shakes her head. "No."

"Danika and Edie had already gone," I say. "I was about to go next and then—well, it felt like someone pushed me, but it could have been an accident."

She bites her lower lip. "I bet I know what you're thinking. Melissa, right?" She turns to watch Melissa, who is stretching on the floor.

I follow her gaze. "Probably," I say.

"Her mom used to be the principal dancer for some big ballet company. Winnipeg, maybe?"

"Yeah, I know." I tilt my head, curious. "Have you met her?"

"No." Mackenzie sighs. "You think she has some influence on who gets the part of Clara? I bet she knows all the people on the panel."

I shift my position. My ankle really hurts and I can't get comfortable. I'm half regretting not staying on the comfortable couch in Edie's living room. "They wouldn't pick Melissa if she was no good," I say. "No matter who her mother is."

"Yeah, but she is good." Mackenzie looks discouraged.

"You're good too." I punch her shoulder lightly. "And at least you can dance. How many Claras have you seen on crutches?"

She rolls her eyes. "Har har."

The sound of clapping hands makes us both look up. Diana is standing in the doorway, her expression serious. "Girls, I'm caught up in a meeting at the moment, so you'll be joining another class this morning. Melissa, can you come with me, please?"

* * *

Everyone is buzzing with questions as we head down the hallway to the other studio. "Why did she want Melissa?" Danika asks. "And where's Edie?"

"I bet they both got the part of Clara," Julie says enviously. "I bet that's what they're meeting about." She holds the door for me, and I hop through.

"Yeah," I say. "Maybe." Or maybe Edie told on Melissa. I find a chair and watch my classmates join the older girls at the barre, but my mind isn't on the dancing.

Then Diana pops her head in the door. "Cassandra? Can you come with me, please?"

My cheeks heat up. *Am I in trouble? Maybe Edie and Melissa have made up some story about me...*My heart is jackhammering in my chest as I hobble down the hallway behind Diana. She gestures me to go into the office ahead of her.

Edie and Melissa are sitting on the couch. Edie is red-eyed and teary, Melissa pale and defiant. Neither of them meets my eyes.

Diana pulls up a chair for me, and I sit down awkwardly. "I want to start by apologizing to you,"

Diana says. "You told me that you weren't responsible for the Facebook post, and I didn't believe you. And now Edie has told me that she made the post. I am sorry, Cassandra."

"It's okay," I say, embarrassed. "I mean, I guess it looked pretty bad."

"Edie?" Diana prompts.

"I'm sorry," Edie says.

"I know." I look at Diana. "She already apologized to me. At home, I mean. But I'm glad you know. I hated having you think I would do that."

Diana clears her throat. "There's one other thing we have to talk about. Edie thinks that Melissa pushed you at the audition. Cassandra, I want you to tell me the truth. Were you pushed? Is that why you fell?"

I hesitate. It is so tempting to say yes...but I don't know. Not for sure. "I didn't see," I admit. "I think someone crashed into me, but I don't know who. And it might not have been on purpose."

"See?" Melissa says. "Edie's just trying to put the blame on me so she doesn't look so bad."

"That's enough, Melissa." Diana looks weary. "You and Edie had better go on to your next class. Cassandra, please stay for a few minutes."

Melissa marches out of the office without a backward glance, but Edie meets my eyes as she gets up, and something—a flash of sympathy or understanding—passes between us.

Diana closes the door behind them and sits back down. "I am so sorry about all of this, Cassandra."

"It's not your fault."

"No, but...I want you to know that we will be keeping a very close eye on things from now on."

It's a bit late, if you ask me.

I don't say it out loud, but Diana reads my thoughts. "I personally will be keeping a close eye on Melissa," she says. "There's no proof that she pushed you, so I don't think we can do anything about that, but from what Edie has told me, Melissa has been something of a bully with not just you but all the new girls."

I nod. "Yeah, you could say that."

There is a long silence. Finally, Diana sighs. "Melissa has been with us since she was four years old. I don't think she's always had an easy time." She looks at me. "Not that there's an excuse for bullying."

"What do you mean?" I ask.

Diana presses one polished fingertip against her lips. "I'm not sure how much I should say.

Has Edie told you anything about Melissa's family?"

"Just that her mother was a famous dancer."

"Yes. She had a very successful career. Melissa's father died about five years ago, so it's just the two of them. And"—she clears her throat—"it is very important to Melissa's mother that her daughter also have a successful career in ballet."

"But that's what Melissa wants anyway," I point out.

"Is it?"

"Of course. Everyone knows that."

Diana gives me a look, and there's something sad about her smile. "I don't know that Melissa has ever had a chance to want anything else." She sighs. "What about you, Cassandra? What do you want?"

"Right now I'd be happy just to be able to dance," I say, gesturing at my crutches. "And, you know, walk."

"What about PTP? If you were offered a spot, would you want to stay?"

"It's not likely now, is it? I won't even be able to dance until the end of the summer."

Diana steeples her hands together and looks at me over her fingertips. "We invite girls into

PTP based on our assessment of their potential, not their current ability. From what I've seen over the past two weeks, you have that potential."

"You mean there's still a chance?" I feel like the sun has just come out after weeks of rain; an energy, a lightness, is rushing through me. I feel like dancing right here and now.

"Definitely. The way you have handled all of this...this unpleasantness with the other girls... shows your character. You've danced well. You haven't allowed yourself to be thrown off or distracted." She meets my eyes and smiles, her head tilted to one side. "You've kept your focus, and you've showed the kind of positive attitude that a dancer needs. That can't have been easy, Cassandra."

I swallow. "No. It hasn't been."

"I suggest that you talk to your parents." Diana stands up. "You should think about what you want. I suspect you're going to need to make a big decision soon."

* * *

I have lunch with Cam and Mackenzie. They're dying to know what happened this morning, and I tell them, but I don't feel like talking about it much. I can't stop thinking about Diana's question to me.

"Would you stay if you got into PTP?" I ask.

"Duh, what do you think?" Cam looks at me like I'm crazy. "Of course I would."

Mackenzie looks thoughtful. "I want to get in," she says, "but I don't think I'd stay. I'd miss my family too much. I've got three brothers, and we're pretty close. Maybe in another year. When I'm fifteen, you know?"

It hadn't occurred to me that this isn't a yes-or-no decision—that not doing it now doesn't mean not doing it ever. If I'm not ready this fall, there's always next year. "Yeah," I say, with a sense of relief. "That makes sense."

"I bet you get in," Cam says to me. "You deserve to. If it's what you want."

I don't tell her that Diana pretty much told me I'd get in. I don't want to brag, and besides, it's not like Diana made any promises. Still, I know I need to make a decision soon.

Living in Canada, on the other side of the world from my family, going to high school here, spending every free minute dancing...

Is this what I want?

Seventeen

That afternoon, Diana makes an announcement. Melissa and Mackenzie have been chosen to play the part of Clara in *The Nutcracker.* Iako is to learn the part as well, in case one of them can't do it for some reason. It's not really a surprise, and I'm thrilled for Mackenzie and Iako.

For Melissa—not so much.

I look around, searching out their faces. Mackenzie has a grin almost as wide as her face and is bouncing up and down on her toes, hugging herself like she can hardly believe it. I wonder what she'll do—if this will make her decide to stay, or if she'll decide to turn it down.

I'm kind of glad I don't have to make that decision.

Then I spot Melissa. She's smiling too, but without any of Mackenzie's exuberance. Her smile looks more like relief than happiness. I wonder if this is what she wants—or if, like Diana suggested, this is more about her mother's ambition than her own.

* * *

As soon as we get home, I ask Edie if I can borrow her laptop to Skype my parents.

"Sure," she says. She seems kind of pale and subdued.

"Are you okay?" I ask her.

"Yeah." She hesitates. "Diana was pretty nice to me, considering."

"She *is* nice." I think for a moment. "I bet she thought it was brave of you, you know? To admit that you did the Facebook thing."

"I guess." She unplugs her computer from where it is recharging on the dining room table. "Here, you can take it to your room. If you want privacy, I mean. You don't have to."

"It's okay," I say. "I knew what you meant." I reach out to take the computer from her, but she doesn't let go. "Edie?"

"I just...I hope you don't hate me now," she says.

"Of course I don't."

"Melissa does," she says.

"She'll get over it."

She shakes her head. "I don't know. She's not even speaking to me." She blinks a few times. "And I really wanted to be Clara."

"There's always next year," I say. "And...um... if Melissa still isn't talking to you next week, you can hang out with me and Cam and Mackenzie at lunch. If you want."

She hands me the laptop. "Thanks, Cassandra."

I head to my room, wondering what possessed me to say that. Shouldn't I be mad? But I'm not, for some reason. I feel like I've aged about five years over the past two weeks though.

I open Skype and call my parents.

While I wait for them to answer, I think about what Diana said about Melissa: *I don't know that Melissa has ever had a chance to want anything else.*

I've always complained about my parents not understanding my love of dancing, always felt frustrated by their insistence that I take time off, not work so hard, have other interests...but maybe all of that has been a good thing.

Maybe it's allowed me to have a choice.

Maybe it's given me the freedom to know what I want.

My mom's face appears on the screen. "Cassie!"

"Hi, Mom," I say.

"How's your ankle? Is everything okay?"

I nod slowly. "Yeah," I tell her. "Everything is really good."

Acknowledgments

Many thanks to Maureen Eastick, ballet teacher and choreographer, for welcoming me into her studio and allowing me to watch as she taught, encouraged and inspired a group of young dancers. Thanks also to Sasha Beardmore, Alyssa Beattie and Sophia Harrington for all their encouragement and suggestions; to Alex Van Tol and Kari Jones for being great writing buddies; and to Sarah Harvey, as always, for being such a fabulous editor and friend.

ROBIN STEVENSON is the author of more than a dozen books for children and teens, including four novels in the Orca Soundings series. Robin spends most of her time writing, hanging out with her son and teaching creative writing to adults, teens and kids. She lives in Victoria, British Columbia, with her family. For more information, please visit www.robinstevenson.com.